COLLINS EDUCATIONAL

Developing Dictionary Skills in French

Martine Pillette

Photocopiable worksheets for use at 11-16 with special emphasis on 16+ examinations

DEVELOPING DICTIONARY SKILLS IN FRENCH

The National Curriculum states that students "should be taught to use dictionaries and reference materials" and students are now entitled to take a dictionary into examinations. Thus, the need for students to use (and not misuse!) a bilingual dictionary has never been more pressing.

* This pack of photocopiable masters provides you with ready-to-use and "fun" activities to develop your students' dictionary skills.

* Examples are taken from Collins Pocket French Dictionary but the materials can be used alongside any reputable bilingual dictionary.

* The easy way to meet the new NC requirements for dictionary usage

* Crosses age ranges and abilities: KS3 and KS4, less able and more able

* Fully photocopiable

* Ideal for use in the classroom or at home

May 1996   0 00 320194-5   48pp   £25.00

Contents
The activities contained in the pack cover a wide range of topic areas and help students to develop a variety of dictionary skills including: learning how a dictionary is organized - finding meanings - mastering phonetics - when not to use a dictionary - using a dictionary in an exam.

ACKNOWLEDGMENTS

The author gratefully acknowledges all those who helped in the writing of this book, especially: Beth Hecker, Beth Treat, Angie Eron, Marie Lynch, Jim Visoskas, and my parents. If I've forgotten anyone, please accept my apologies.

CHAPTER ONE

"I want you to find my dead husband."

"Excuse me?" That was my first reaction.

"I want you to find my husband. He's dead, and I need to know where he is." She spoke in a voice one sexy note below middle C.

"Uh-huh." That was my second reaction. Really slick.

Moments before, when I saw her standing in the outer room, waiting to come into my office, I had the feeling she'd be trouble. And now, with that intro, I knew it.

"He's dead, and I need you to find him." If she wasn't tired of the repetition, I was, but I couldn't seem to get my mouth working. She sat in the cushy black leather chair on the other side of my desk, exhaling money with every sultry breath. She had beautiful blond hair with just a hint of darker color at the roots, blue eyes like a cold mountain lake, and a smile that would slay Adonis. I'd like to say that a beautiful woman couldn't influence me by her beauty alone. I'd like to say it, but I can't.

"Why didn't you come see me yesterday?" I asked. Her eyes

1

widened in surprise. This detective misses nothing, I thought, mentally patting myself on the back. She didn't know that I'd definitely noticed her yesterday eating at a deli across the street. I had been staring out the window, and there she was.

The shoulders of her red designer jacket went up a half-inch and back down, then her full lips curled into the trace of a smile. "I came here to see you, but you were leaving for lunch. I followed you, and then I lost my nerve."

"I see you've regained it." I've never been one to place too much importance on my looks, but I suddenly wished I could run a comb through my hair, put on a nicer shirt, and splash on a little cologne. And change my eye color – hazel – boring. It sounded like someone's old, spinster aunt, not an eye color.

She nodded. "Yes. I have to find out about my husband. He's dead, I know it. I just know it." Her tone swayed as if in a cool breeze, with no hint of the desperation that should've been carried in the words.

"But he's also missing," I said in a tone bordering on flippant, as I leaned forward to unlock the desk drawer where I kept spare change, paper clips, and my favorite gold pen. Maybe writing things down would help me concentrate. But I caught a whiff of something elegant coming from her direction, and the key I was holding missed the lock by a good two inches. I hoped she didn't see my blunder. I felt my face getting warm and assumed my cheeks were turning crimson. I hoped she didn't see that either.

Perhaps I was being too glib because she glanced back toward the door as if she had mistaken my office for another. "This is the Ferguson Detective Agency? You are Reed Ferguson?"

"It is and I am." I smiled in my most assured manner, then immediately questioned what I was doing. This woman was making no sense and here I was, flirting with her like a high-school jock. I glanced behind her at the framed movie poster from the *The Big Sleep*, starring Humphrey Bogart and Lauren Bacall. It was one of my favorites, and I hung the poster in my office as a sort of inspiration. I wanted to be as cool as Bogie. I wondered what he would do right now.

She puckered pink lips at me. "I need your help."

"That's what I'm here for." Now I sounded cocky.

The pucker turned into a fully developed frown. "I'm very serious, Mr. Ferguson."

"Reed." I furrowed my brow and looked at my potential first client with as serious an expression as I could muster. I noticed for the first time that she applied her makeup a bit heavy, in an attempt to cover blemishes.

"Reed," she said. "Let me explain." Now we were getting somewhere. I found the gold pen, popped the top off it and scrounged around another drawer for a notepad. "My name is Amanda Ghering." She spoke in an even tone, bland, like she was reading a grocery list. "My husband, Peter, left on a business trip three weeks ago yesterday. He was supposed to return on Monday, but he didn't."

Today was Thursday. I wondered what she'd been doing since Monday. "Did you report this to the police?"

She raised a hand to stop me. "Please. I already have and they gave me the standard response, 'Give it some time, he'll show up.' "

That one puzzled me. The police wouldn't file a missing persons case for twenty-four hours, but after that, I was certain they would do something more. "They didn't do anything?"

"They asked me some questions, said they would make a few calls to the airlines." Amanda paused. "They were more concerned about my relationship with Peter," she said, gazing out the window behind me. The only thing she would see was an incredible view of a renovated warehouse across the street.

For a brief moment, her face was flushed in as deep a sadness as I'd ever seen. Then it was gone, replaced by a foggy look when she turned back to me. "You see, Peter wasn't exactly what you'd call a faithful husband." She frowned, creating wrinkles on an otherwise perfect face. "Well, that's not completely true. He was faithful, to his libido at least. But not to our marriage." I paraphrased the last couple of sentences on the notepad. "He travels quite a bit with his company, computer consulting, so he has ample opportunity to dally. And he never tries hard to conceal what he's doing."

"Did you tell the police all of this?"

"Yes. I believe that's why they're not doing that much. That, and the fact that there appears to be no foul play, has kept them from doing little more than paperwork."

"You're afraid they're not treating his disappearance seriously."

"Exactly."

I scratched my chin with the pen. "I'd have to disagree with you about that." I didn't have much experience – okay I didn't have any experience – but in the tons of detective books I'd read and all the movies I'd seen the police would take someone of Amanda's obvious wealth with some concern. At least until she gave them a reason not to.

"They don't have the resources to track him down," she countered. "That's left up to me, which is what I'm here to do."

"And this way you also keep any nasty details private."

"Exactly."

"Why come to me?"

Amanda glanced around the sparsely furnished office and the stark white walls decorated with nothing more than movie posters, as if she were second-guessing her choice of detectives. "You came recommended. I know you're not licensed but..."

"You don't have to be in the state of Colorado," I interrupted. Anyone who wanted to could be a detective here, just hang up a sign. Hell, you didn't even need a gun. I could testify to that. Never had one, never shot one.

She waved a hand at me. "I don't care if you're licensed or not. I know your background. You come from a well-to-do family; you know when to be discreet."

I came recommended. Now that caught my curiosity. The only thing I'd done was to help a wealthy friend of my father track down an old business partner. It was slightly dangerous but not noteworthy, and at the time I didn't have an office or a business. I had been between jobs, so I decided to pursue an old dream. I hung up a shingle to try my hand at detecting. I loved old detective novels, had read everything from Rex Stout and Dashiell Hammett to Raymond Chandler and James M. Cain. I'd watched Humphrey Bogart, William Powell, and all the classic film noir movies. I pictured myself just like those great detectives. Well, maybe not. But I was going to try.

"Who recommended me?" I asked. The list was surely small.

"A friend at my club."

"Really? Who?"

"Paul Burrows. Do you know him?"

I shook my head. "Does he know my father?" I assumed he was someone who'd heard about me helping my father's friend.

"I don't know, but Paul said you were good, and that you could use the work."

She was right about that. I lived comfortably off an inheritance from my obscenely rich grandparents, plus some smart investments I'd made over the years, so I'd never had a real career. I had always wanted to work in law enforcement, but my parents had talked me out of that. Instead, I got a law degree, flitted from job to job, and disappointed my father because I never stuck with anything. I hoped being a detective would change all that; it was something I'd always wanted to do, but my father still thought I was playing around. I needed to solve a real case to prove him wrong.

"Are you a fan of old movies?" Amanda asked, noticing the posters for the first time.

I nodded. "I like old movies, but especially detective film noir."

"Film noir?"

I pointed to a different poster on another wall of *The Maltese Falcon*, one of Bogie's most famous movies. "Movies with hard-boiled detectives, dark themes, and dark characters."

"And dark women?" Amanda said.

I kept a straight face as I gazed at Lauren Bacall. "Yeah, that too."

"I hope you're as good as Sam Spade," Amanda said.

I watched her cross one shapely leg over the other, her red wool skirt edging up her thigh. Trouble. Just like I'd thought before. I should have run out of my own office, but I didn't. I know what you're thinking, it's her beauty. No, it was what she said next that complicated things immensely.

"I'm prepared to pay whatever it takes." Saying that, she pulled a stack of bills from her purse. I crossed my arms and contemplated her. This sounded like I'd just be chasing after a philandering husband. Not exciting at all, even though I had little basis for making that assumption, other than what I'd read in books. But a voice inside my head said that making money meant it was a real job, right?

I named my daily wage, plus expenses. It was top dollar, but she didn't blink. And I had my first real case. What would my father say to that?

———

"Let's start with you clarifying a couple of things," I said. Moments before Amanda had inked her name on a standard contract, officially making her my first client. "How do you know your husband's dead and not just missing?"

Amanda sighed. "Because he would've called me, kept in touch, and I haven't heard a word from him."

"But if he was out with someone else?"

She shook her head. "No, he always calls. He pretends things are normal. We have our routine and he always follows it. Only this time he didn't."

"But he knew?"

"That I knew?"

I nodded. She nodded. "Yes, he knew."

I resisted the urge to continue the Dr. Seuss rhyme. "So he hasn't called you, but what makes you jump to the conclusion that his not calling means he's dead?" I leaned back in my chair, tipping it up on two legs. "What if he wanted to disappear, or he's fallen in love with someone else and has run off with her?"

Amanda emitted a very unladylike snort. "Peter's not capable of love, so it's impossible for him to leave me. Not for that reason, anyway."

"Have you given him another reason to leave?"

She hesitated. "I was going to kill him."

We moved out of the realm of boring. The chair legs hit the floor hard. "Excuse me?"

"I was going to kill him," she repeated. She stared down at her hands and ticked items off on an index finger. "For the insurance money and the inheritance. Well over five million. Besides that, I would get my freedom from the farce of our marriage." She spoke matter-of-factly, as if she were detailing a cooking recipe. "I was trying to figure out a way to do it. I couldn't make it look like a suicide, because I'd lose out on the insurance money. I couldn't murder him, because I couldn't guarantee getting away with it, and I might not get any money that way either. A domestic dispute gone bad was out of the question because Peter wouldn't hit a rabid dog, let alone his wife. I was left with creating an accident. Only I never could figure out what to do. Help him lose control and drive off a snowy mountain road? Too much risk for me. Electric shock of some sort? But how could I pull that off? Poison? But with what, and how to keep it from being discovered?" Her breasts lifted and sank in a deep sigh. "I finally gave up," she said and looked me straight in the eye. "I didn't do anything."

Blurting out her plans like that intrigued me. Bogie never had it this easy. "But he's disappeared," I came back to the original point. "How do I know that you didn't have him killed?"

"Why would I hire you?"

"To make it look like you weren't involved."

She smiled. "I'm afraid that's impossible. First of all, I wouldn't know where to start. And as I said, I gave up the idea of killing him."

"Then how do you know he's dead? If he knew you wanted him dead, that's a lot of motivation not to come home."

"He didn't know anything about it."

"But you just said that he might not come home because he knew you were trying to kill him."

She emitted an exasperated sigh. "Peter never knew anything," she said again.

"How do you know?"

She spoke to me like I was the class dunce. "All Peter knew was that our marriage, and his money, were in jeopardy. When I was considering what I might do to him, I was less," she struggled to find the right words, "less than kind to him. Cold. Indifferent. He sensed that. Then I decided I was being foolish, so I resumed the game. Things were back to normal, whatever that was. He didn't have any reason not to come home."

I sat back again, feeling like I'd missed the answer to a test question. "So I'm supposed to find your presumably dead husband, whom you wanted to kill, but deny that you did, and now that he's gone, you want him back."

"Yes," she said, exasperated.

"Fine," I said.

I should've run, right then. I should've, but I didn't.

CHAPTER TWO

"This is quite a house," I said as Amanda walked out of her huge three-car garage. I noticed a black Porsche parked in the far space, and a blue Mercedes in the middle spot, next to Amanda's sleek gray Lexus.

I had just followed Amanda to her house in Castle Pines, an exclusive gated community of huge, custom-built homes resting in the shadows of the Rocky Mountains near Castle Rock. The continuing sprawl of suburban Denver threatened smaller towns, but in areas like Castle Pines, between Castle Rock and south Denver, the neighborhoods were still quiet and you had breathtaking views of the mountains thrown in. I could smell fresh pine carried in an early winter breeze that whipped up dead leaves in the lawn.

"Come on inside," she said, looking around nervously. I didn't know what she had to worry about; the nearest house was at least a hundred feet away and I hadn't seen anybody out on the meandering road that led to her place.

I suppressed a whistle as we walked across creamy red flag-stone steps to a long front porch. Having grown up in the cradle of wealth, I was not easily impressed, but this came close. The Ghering house, with its opulent Victorian design, certainly challenged my childhood home in size. It was painted eggshell white, complemented by black trim and decorative ironwork on the windows, with a huge red brick chimney jutting out from the south side of the house. Unlit Christmas lights hung from the eave, and from the branches of two large pine trees in the front yard.

"Why did you give up the idea of killing Peter?" I asked as we stepped inside. A spacious foyer branched off in three directions, to the right a cozy sitting room, to the left a large living room, lavishly decorated, and straight ahead stairs leading to the second floor. It didn't take a detective to know that a lot of money had gone into the decor.

"Let me take your coat," Amanda said, hanging both hers and mine in a closet under the staircase. "Would you like a drink?"

I hesitated because it was barely lunchtime. "It's a bit early for me. A glass of water would be fine. And how about an answer to my question."

She beckoned me to follow her into the living room, where she crossed to a minibar and began preparing drinks, water and ice for me, vodka and a splash of Rose's lime juice for her. I curled an eyebrow at her as she swallowed half her drink. "This whole thing's got me tied up in knots," she said, justifying her actions.

I sat down on an expensive leather sofa near a towering Christmas tree adorned with gold ribbons and red lights. I sipped my glass of water and said nothing, but wondered if she'd already thrown back a drink or two before coming to my office. It could explain her willingness to talk.

Amanda stared at me as she finished her drink. "I decided not to kill Peter because he may be unfaithful, but he's not worth killing." She set the empty glass back on the bar and pushed an imaginary hair away from her eyes. As she talked, I was riveted by those eyes, how piercing they were. "I assumed the role of the spoiled rich wife, a country club woman," she continued, toying with an enormous diamond on her left ring finger that reflected the light from a huge bay window. "I use his money like he uses me. I'm a side attraction, there when he wants me; I fade into the woodwork when he doesn't."

Dressed as she was in another expensive designer outfit, every piece from her earrings to the matching leather heels, she clearly used his money well. "Tell me about this business trip," I said, sinking further into the sofa.

"Peter started out in Florida. He stayed there for a week, then a week in New York, and he was supposed to be in Philadelphia this last week."

"Supposed to be? Did he not make it to Philadelphia?"

"No."

"Are you sure?"

Amanda frowned. "Of course I'm sure. The last time I heard from Peter was his last night in New York. He was leaving for Philly the next morning. The police told me that his ticket from New York to Philly wasn't used."

"Could he have changed his mind? Taken the train instead?"

"I suppose that's possible. But it isn't like Peter. He's meticulous to a fault and tied to his routines. I can't see him changing his plans like that and not telling me."

"Okay, so he didn't use the airline ticket, and you didn't hear from him this past week." I cocked my head to the side. "But that doesn't mean he never made it to Philadelphia. Or that he's dead."

"True." She thrust a finger in my direction. "That's why I hired you, to find out what happened. I think he's dead. Maybe he had an accident, met an angry husband of one of his lovers. I don't know, but I'm preparing myself for the worst." She was doing a fine job of it, I thought, eyeing the empty glass behind her.

"Then you'd inherit the money and all your problems would be solved."

Her face twisted into a quick mixture of emotions – sadness, pleasure, fear, then blank. "I suppose. Boy, would that make Peter's parents angry."

"Why?"

Amanda contemplated the question for a moment, then said, "Peter's parents never really liked me. I think they resent the fact that Peter has done well for himself, that we live so well now. They don't live as well, but money from Peter's estate would go a long way for them."

"You're sure you would inherit and not his parents?"

"Yes. I saw a copy of the will after Peter came from the attorney's office. His parents have their own money. Not as much as us, but they have some. He didn't see any need to give them any more."

I pondered her last revelation. "I can see why you hope he's dead."

If it angered her, she didn't show it. She stood a bit straighter and gazed at me, unflappable. We stayed in speculative silence long enough for me to sing the chorus of The Police's "Murder by Numbers" in my head.

"So," I finally said. I set my empty glass on the coffee table and leaned my elbows on my knees. "Do you have a copy of Peter's itinerary and who he was working for?"

"Sure."

"Plane reservations, hotel reservations, any car rental information?"

She nodded. "All of that should be upstairs in his office. Peter was self-employed, so everything would be there."

"Let's have a look," I said.

"Right now?"

"Is that okay?" I asked. I wondered about the slight resistance, but dismissed it.

"No, that's fine." I stood up and followed Amanda as she headed for the stairs, passing a picture in a gold frame sitting on a teak wood end table. "Is this Peter?" I asked, picking up the photo.

Amanda stopped and turned. "Yes. As you can see, he's easy to fall for. Tall, six-two; dark brown eyes, quite good-looking," Amanda said. I examined the picture and agreed. Peter Ghering, dressed in white shorts and a dark blue Oxford shirt, stood in front of a long white sailboat, a cocky half-smile on his tanned face. He kept his hair short, the curls neatly slicked into place. He pointed at the camera with his sunglasses, seeming relaxed, a man without a care in the world.

"How recent is this?" I asked.

"Taken last summer, but he still looks the same."

"Six to eight months probably wouldn't change him much," I said, memorizing the picture before I put the photo back. "What kind of a man is Peter?" I chose my words with care, speaking of him in the present. No reason to think otherwise.

"A control freak, driven to succeed. Highly successful, but emotionally he has nothing to give. He's charming, at least at times, devastatingly handsome, and great in bed. That alone kept me going for a long time."

A Harlequin hero. "How long have you been married?"

"Fifteen years." Amanda gazed out the window, as if she could see her wedding day in the sunshine outside. "We were young, right out of college. Peter was going places and I wanted to be right there with him. He liked the high life, and so did I. We were going to be Mr. and Mrs. Perfect." Her eyes turned back to me. "But the monotony of marriage set in. He spent

15

more time on business trips; I spent more time at the country club. He began to play around."

"Did you?"

"Have an affair?"

I nodded.

"No," she said. "Tempted, once, but I didn't. When I wanted great sex, I had Peter. As for an affair, I never met anyone that I thought could be a suitable companion."

That made sense, at least at the moment. "Was he always unfaithful?"

"I didn't think so, but looking back on it, he probably was. A few of my sorority sisters were awfully close with him. At the time I was in love, so I didn't see anything bad in their behavior. I assumed he was being friendly."

"Any children?"

"None. I wanted to, but he didn't."

"Any financial troubles? Business troubles?"

"No," she said. "Everything was great. We were playing the game like we always did, no questions asked. Then Peter didn't call. It doesn't fit. He should've come home."

I wondered why a man with no problems would disappear. Unless she was the problem. The threat of a violent end at the hands of one's wife seemed like a problem to me. If he knew about it.

Amanda turned to head upstairs to Peter's office. "I know you don't believe Peter's dead. Please, find out what happened to him. I need to know."

With five million hanging in the balance, I could see why.

CHAPTER THREE

Peter's office took up the whole north side of the house. The room was painted a light, creamy brown, with large windows east and west. A mahogany desk the size of a compact car sat directly across from the door, taking up a sizable portion of the room. On one side of it was a two drawer file cabinet, on the other a computer printer sitting on a small stand. Three-foot shelves spanned the entire wall behind the desk, and a huge painting of a sailboat on calm waters hung centered on the wall over the desk. In the remainder of the room were a small table with a reading chair in one corner and a glass display case with a few model boats in the other corner.

"This is where he works," Amanda said. "When he's in town," she said as an afterthought.

I moved around the desk and sat in the leather executive chair. Definitely more comfortable than the one in my office; it cushioned my underside like a pillow. I ran my hands across the mahogany desktop, then checked out the computer monitor. It was the very latest model, practically paper thin, taking up very little room on the desk. I lightly tapped the keyboard, then switched on a small antique Tiffany desk lamp. The room reeked of expensive taste.

"He also has a laptop for travel," Amanda said. "It's with him."

That made sense, since he was on a business trip, but I didn't point out the obvious. "I guess we have to start here. Do you mind if I look at what he's got on the computer?"

"I could care less what's on that thing." I glanced at her as I turned it on. Did she despise the technology or the man who used it?

"Let's see what we have here." I waited for the computer to think its way through initial setup; when it finished, the desktop appeared with a variety of files on it. I examined them, humming the catchy opening notes from a tune by The Smiths. I double-clicked on one file after another. Most of the files were documents related to Peter's work, details of program modifications, suggestions for improvements, and a lot of computer lingo that I didn't understand. A few documents prompted me for a password, which raised my curiosity. Not that they contained anything more than contracts or something he wouldn't want just anybody, like me, to have access to, but a detective didn't like not knowing.

"Anything interesting?" Amanda asked after a bit of fidgeting from the reading chair.

"Nope." I continued perusing files and humming The Smiths song.

"Is that *How Soon Is Now?*" she asked.

I looked up in surprise. "Sure is." Not too many people recognized that alternative '80s band, or one of their greatest hits.

"I think we're about the same age," she said with a roll of her eyes. "You're what? Thirty? Thirty-five?"

"Thirty-four," I said.

"Class of eighty-two." Amanda smiled. "I like a lot of the groups from the eighties."

"The Smiths were great," I said, feeling like the schoolboy again. She likes the same music as I do! Get a grip, Reed. She's a client. But I kept humming.

"Well, well. What have we here?"

Amanda bolted up from the chair and came around the desk. "What?"

I was checking Peter's emails. I couldn't believe he hadn't password protected them, but it made my job easier. The Inbox contained only a few, but one of those was from a lady named Sheila. The email was dated six months ago, and was brief but to the point.

"Dear Peter," it read. "So glad to hear from you. Call me when you get in and we can have dinner and then... :-)". Below that: "Love Sheila". Underneath that was an auto signature, standard with most company emails, and this conveniently listed her full name as Sheila Banks. It also had the company address, phone and fax numbers, and web site address. Sheila obviously had little concern about being caught. Either that, or she was incredibly stupid. I'd recently heard about a couple who had spent the night together, and the unfortunate woman wrote her lover a steamy email about their night of passion, only to see him send it on to his friends, who send it on to their friends, and so on. In a nanosecond the email passed through cyberspace, ending up in Inboxes all over the world, turning into a lover's nightmare. I saw the story on the news. I'll bet Sheila didn't count on Peter keeping her email around, which wasn't a very smart assumption on her part.

"That jerk," Amanda said, smacking a delicate palm on the desk. "Keeping an email like that. I knew they were contacting him, but to keep the evidence..." I knew exactly who "they" were. And it sounded like there were a lot of "them."

"Where did you expect them to contact him?"

She bit her lip. "I don't know. I guess when he got to whatever city they were in. Not here."

"Maybe Peter didn't consider his computer part of your home." I pulled out a pad and pen from my coat pocket while I talked. "However, I would've thought he'd at least keep the correspondence on his laptop and not here." I printed the email, complete with Sheila's business information and email address.

"Why?" Amanda asked. "I never use this computer. As a matter of fact, I hardly use the computer Peter bought me, except for occasional emails to keep up with friends."

"But you could've looked here."

Amanda shook her head. "No, it's like I told you. Peter and I kept up the pretense of a good marriage. I had no need to spy on him. Besides, I knew what was going on. There wouldn't be any need for me to look here at all."

The other emails were business correspondence, but I jotted down names and addresses just in case. I didn't find anything else on the computer that seemed significant, so I shut it down and rummaged around in the desk drawers. "Where's his itinerary?"

"Right here." Amanda opened the file cabinet drawer and pulled out a manila folder marked "airline info", and handed it to me.

I leaned back in the chair and thumbed through the papers. Each was a travel printout either from a travel agent or an airline, organized chronologically, with the latest trip in the back. On his apparent last trip, Peter flew United Airlines, starting out twenty-six days ago. The printout detailed flight information and times from Miami, Florida, to New York City, and then Philadelphia.

"Three weeks. That's a long business trip."

She shrugged. "That was where the work was, so he took it. He made great money by consulting."

I closed the file. "Can I take this with me?" Amanda nodded, so I set the file aside and examined the rest of the folders in the cabinet.

"Here's his hotel information," I said, pulling out another folder neatly labeled like the others. I shuffled through it. The last sheet was an email printout from a travel agent showing which hotels Peter was booked in and for how many nights, the last in Philadelphia. I put that aside as well.

I looked further, admiring the neat and organized manner in which Peter kept his business files. I did not have nearly the talent. I found folders for each trip he had taken from the beginning of the year, ten months worth, with receipts and an itemized printout recording each expense in detail. Planes, hotels, taxis, parking, car rental, all paper clipped to the print out. The last folder had a label with the dates of this trip, but it was empty, the receipts Peter would have collected presumably still with him, wherever he was.

"Too bad," I said. "But at least I've got names of hotels where he planned to stay. That's a starting point."

"Yes."

"Did the police check with any of them?"

She shrugged her shoulders. "I don't know. I talked to them yesterday, and they didn't tell me anything."

"Who's the detective working on this?"

"His name is Detective Merrick. Jimmy Merrick. He's with the Douglas County Sheriff's Department."

I took down his phone number and made a mental note to contact him, then rummaged some more, checking all the drawers. More letters to clients, marketing plans, bills. That was all. Enough to know that Peter made a lot of money, but little else. I opened the thin middle drawer of the desk, pushed around the papers and notepads, uncovering some photos. I pulled them out, four in all. In each one Peter posed with a different woman, and from the backgrounds, in different locations. The women were stunningly gorgeous and appeared to be much younger than Peter. He hadn't tried very hard to hide his dalliances.

I handed them to Amanda. "Recognize any of them?"

As she looked at them, her breathing became more controlled, heavy breaths coming out of a slit in her mouth. "No." She slapped them on the desk. "No, I don't recognize them."

"You don't know anything about his liaisons?"

"No. I told you, we pretended everything was normal." I wondered how she could keep up the pretense when he had so much available time and seemingly so many available women.

"Do you mind if I take these?" I picked up the pictures.

"What do I want with them?" she murmured with a dismissive wave of her hand.

I sat back in the chair and slowly looked around the room, searching for inspiration, something to set off a flame. I didn't even get a spark. Only the silence of the room, and the low rumblings of a huge, nearly empty house.

"So what do you do now?" Amanda broke the quiet.

I shrugged. "Try and track Peter down through hotel records, that sort of thing. See where this email leads." I held up the stack of papers.

"If you need anything else, let me know."

"I do need one other thing."

She tucked a wave of hair behind her ear, waiting for me to continue. "I'm assuming you have shared credit cards?" She nodded. "Good. I need you to call them or go online and get the transaction information for the past three weeks. I want to know all the transactions, when and where. As soon as you can get it."

"I can do that this afternoon. Will that be quick enough?"

"Sure," I said. "You can call me at the office."

"Is that all?"

I smiled. "For now."

She leaned against the edge of the desk. "If you're done here, how would you like to have a drink before you go?"

Was she flirting with me? No, couldn't be. I tried to look at my watch without looking like I was looking at my watch.

"I know it's early," she rushed to explain, leaning forward. "But I'm used to having a cocktail at the club with lunch."

I caught another whiff of perfume. "No, uh, thanks." I stood up but Amanda didn't budge.

"Do you know why I hired you?" She traced a figure eight on the desk. Back and forth.

"Because I can be discreet?"

One side of her mouth turned up in a sexy half-smile. "Yes. And you seem like a nice guy." A cliché, but it worked. I felt my chest getting tight.

"It's just one drink."

"I don't think that's a good idea," I said.

"Well, maybe another time." The half smile remained.

I tripped around the desk. "I'd better be going."

A pout formed at the corners of her mouth. "If you say so." She continued to trace on the desk. "Will you take a rain check?"

"Sure," I agreed. And got the hell out of there.

CHAPTER FOUR

My office, creatively named "Ferguson Detective Agency", occupies two small rooms in a renovated warehouse in downtown Denver, a few blocks from the outdoor Sixteenth Street Mall, the city's urban heartbeat. The rent borders on outrageous, but I thrive on the lively atmosphere and the burgeoning nightlife in the neighborhood. I also like that I have my very own bathroom; it's miniscule, but at least I don't have to run to the end of the hall every time nature calls. Or when I need to splash water on my face.

"Wow. That's cold," I said to my reflection in the mirror above the sink in the bathroom. My hazel eyes gazed back, chastising me. I had just successfully averted a liaison with my first client. At least for the moment.

"Focus, Reed. It's your first case," I said to my reflection. "You don't want to emulate *all* the traits of the movie detectives." Like having an affair with your client, who also happens to be married.

I dried my face off, feeling more-or-less in control. I tossed the towel on a rung and returned to the office. Okay, what would Bogie do, I asked myself as I paced back and forth.

After a moment I sat down at my desk, grabbed the phone, and dialed a hotel number from Peter's itinerary.

"Thank you for calling the Hilton Miami. How may I direct your call?" A deep male voice droned.

"I'm trying to track down a friend of mine who stayed there a couple of weeks ago. Could you help me?" I asked. I've found that a direct approach usually gets you the information you want, and what better way to verify how far Peter had made it through his trip than to contact the hotels on his itinerary?

"Name please." This operator at the Hilton in Miami didn't waste any air.

I figured he was asking for the name of my supposed friend, not me. "Peter Ghering." I spelled it for him.

I heard some tapping on a computer keyboard. "Yes. He stayed here for six nights and left on November twentieth." It's amazing what information can be gleaned from a quick phone call. If you don't hesitate and sound self-assured, you can get almost anything out of anybody.

I thanked him and called the next stop on Peter's itinerary, the Embassy Suites Hotel in New York City. "Could you spell the last name, sir?" a friendly female voice requested.

I did and waited while she looked up the information.

"I'm sorry, sir, but Mr. Ghering checked out over a week ago, on Sunday."

"Did he leave any forwarding information?"

She paused. "No, I'm sorry. Is there anything else I can help you with?"

"No, thanks." I hung up, dialed the number for the hotel in Philadelphia, and went through the same routine.

"Ghering?" another feminine voice asked. "I show that he checked out on Friday morning."

"Any forwarding information?"

"I don't show anything."

I hung up. So Peter Ghering *had* made it to Philadelphia, stayed the week, and left. Where did he go? I read through the itinerary again. It showed that Peter had a flight out of Philadelphia International Airport at just past nine in the morning this past Monday. So what did he do over the weekend, and where did he stay? He was probably with a girlfriend, but which one? And why didn't he use the airline ticket from New York to Philly? Did he not like the puddle-jumpers?

I picked up the phone again and called the number for United Airlines, and after a series of transfers, spoke to a manager.

"This is Abe Avery," a nasally voice said. I pictured Abe speaking with a clothes pin on his nose. "How may I help you?"

I launched into an explanation about how I was trying to find out if the tickets Peter purchased had indeed been used.

"May I have your name please?"

"Sam Spade. I'm a private investigator."

"I'm sorry, Mr. Spade, but that information is confidential." His tone implied that I should've known that.

"This is a missing-persons case," I put an imperative edge in my voice. "This man has not been seen since last Friday."

"I'm sorry, but I cannot reveal that information without a warrant." His voice droned like an annoying bee. "If you'd like to come down here with that, I'm sure I can help you with what you need."

The real Sam Spade didn't have to go through this, I thought. Too bad the airlines weren't as easy as hotels. I thanked Abe anyway and hung up.

My stomach growled, noting that feeding time had passed. I glanced at the clock: two o'clock. At least I'd miss the lunch rush. I walked to BD's Mongolian Grill where a light crowd filled a few tables. Two trips to the make-your-own stir-fry meat, vegetable, and condiments bar filled me up, and I headed back to the office with renewed vigor.

———

When I returned to the office, I checked my voice mail, hoping that Amanda had called with the transaction information from their credit cards, but there were no messages. I decided to see if I could find out anything about the official investigation, so I picked up the phone and called Detective Merrick at the Douglas County Sheriff's Office, located south of Denver.

"Merrick," he said pleasantly into the phone. I identified who I was and my interest in the case. "I see," he said when I'd finished. "I don't envy you your job."

"Excuse me?"

"Nothing," he mumbled. "I really shouldn't divulge any information about our investigation."

"Could you tell me if his airline ticket was used all the way to Denver?" I knew I'd never get this information from the airlines themselves.

He sighed into the phone. "You could get Amanda to look into that."

"I could, but I've got you on the phone."

After a long pause, he said, "The ticket Peter booked was used only as far as Philadelphia. Not back to Denver."

"Did he fly back to Denver on any flight?"

"He wasn't ticketed on any flight that we know of. That doesn't mean he couldn't have taken an unregistered flight, hired a private plane or something like that, but we don't have a record of that. Now that's all you'll get from me." The line went dead.

I sat back in my chair. Amanda told me that Peter's ticket

wasn't used from New York City to Philadelphia. Merrick said that it was. Was she getting things confused? Or was she lying to me?

I grabbed the phone again and called Amanda, but after four rings, an answering machine picked up. I hoped that meant she was working on the credit card information. Or maybe she had sought out the drink at the club. As the digital voice instructed me to leave a message, I wondered why Amanda said what she did about the airline tickets. She had some explaining to do. I heard a beep on the line, asked her to call me when she got in, left my number, and cradled the phone.

I pulled out the sheet of paper with Sheila's email address. I re-booted up my computer, connected to my email, and composed a message to Peter's clandestine friend.

"Sheila," I wrote. "Please contact me about P. Ghering. It's very important. Thanks." I signed it Reed Ferguson, with only my office and cell phone numbers beneath. Unless Sheila was psychic, she would have no idea who I was. I hoped the mystery would prompt a response, but not create too much curiosity in case someone else read Sheila's email. After all, I knew nothing at all about this woman. She might be married or in a relationship. I didn't want to let her secret, however much there was, out of the bag, at least not yet. I'd see what kind of response I got from her first. If this didn't work, I'd resort to a phone call. I hit the send button. "C'mon Sheila, you're a curious woman, right?"

I picked up the four photos of Peter and his nameless girlfriends. Was one of them Sheila? I looked at them more closely. They all had the same general appearance, tall, thin brunettes with long, straight hair, and lots of gold jewelry. Smiles adorned their faces as they clung to Peter while he grinned as if he'd just won the lottery. Cookie-cutter girlfriends. And they bore no resemblance to Amanda.

A sound clip I had downloaded from *The Maltese Falcon,* Bogie's voice, said, "Somebody always gives me guns." When I heard his voice, I knew I had mail. I opened up the message, a cryptic note from Sheila.

"Who are you and what do you want?" the lone line stared back at me.

"So you want to be evasive," I said to the screen. "Okay, you asked for it." I hit the reply button and wrote, "I'm a private investigator. I've been hired by Mrs. Ghering to find the where-abouts of Peter Ghering, and I need to know if you have any information about where he might be, or if you've seen him in the last three weeks." I hit the send button.

"You have to respond now," I said to the screen. "You don't want to be involved, but now you have to know who I am and if I'm telling the truth." While I waited, I turned on my MP3 player and selected The Smiths greatest hits CD. I forwarded it to *"How Soon Is Now"*, sat back down at my desk and sang along. I didn't make it through the song before Bogie's voice inter-rupted. Sheila was hooked.

I opened the email. "Please," it read. "I can't tell you anything right now. I'll call you when I get off work, around six, four your time." I assumed she guessed I was writing from the same city as the Gherings, and that I was in the Mountain Time zone. If she was two hours ahead of me, she lived somewhere on the East coast. New York, Philly, or some other place Peter visited? I responded, telling her to call the office number, and sent the email. I sat back with a satisfied sigh. It was three-thirty. I didn't have long before I'd hear personally from the mysterious Sheila.

CHAPTER FIVE

At precisely four o'clock, my phone rang. I picked it up after a not-to-appear-too-anxious three rings. "Start talking," I said in a way I imagined the inimitable detective Kinky Friedman would talk, to the point and don't waste my time.

"Reed Ferguson?" At any other time the voice would have sounded pleasant, soft and lilting. Right now it sounded like an old beeper on vibrate, all nervous edges.

"And you're Sheila?" I asked.

A pause. "Yes." The connection crackled, mixed with the humming of a car engine. "I'm on my way home from work. This is the only time I can talk to you." No questions about Peter, me, or why I was contacting her.

"Then let's get right to the point," I said. "Tell me about Peter Ghering. Specifically about you and Peter."

"I worked with him on occasion. And before we go any further, how did you get my email address?" A touch of indignation.

"Off of Peter's computer, at his house. And it wasn't a business email." I didn't mention that she'd left all her business identification on a very personal email.

Silence, long enough, I imagined, for her to mentally review her correspondence with Peter, and to wonder if Amanda had read any of it. I began to wonder if the connection had broken when she spoke, the ire gone from her voice.

"I just said, I worked with Peter. That doesn't mean a person can't send a friendly note once in a while."

How stupid did she think I was? "The tone indicated more than words were exchanged," I said. "Why don't you tell me about your relationship with Peter?"

"What do you want to know?"

Now how do you like that! She wanted to play it as if we were exchanging beauty tips. I sat up in my chair, leaning my elbows on the edge of the desk. "Sheila, how long before you get home?"

"What? Uh, in about fifteen minutes."

"Is there a husband waiting for you there?"

Another pause. "Please, you can't let him know anything about this. I can't have that happen."

"Then answer my questions straight and maybe we won't have to involve him." I was all pleasant, but the threat dug deep. "I couldn't care less about your affair. I'm trying to find Peter."

"All right," she said, her voice tight. "I met Peter about a year ago. He was doing some consulting work for my company, and he was out here for a week."

"Where's here?" I asked.

"Willow Grove. A suburb of Philadelphia."

"What happened?"

"We worked through the week, and the last night Peter was here, I took him to dinner. It's standard practice for the company, a courtesy kind of thing. The VP who was supposed

32

to go with us canceled at the last minute, so it was just Peter and me." I heard the sound of a horn honking. "Hey, watch it," Sheila yelled at another driver, then to me in a quiet voice, "Oh, sorry."

I relaxed some and smiled. "No problem." I can relate to rush hour traffic.

"Anyway, we went to dinner, and afterward Peter invited me up to his room for a drink. My husband was out of town, so I said yes. One thing led to another. Do I need to paint you a picture?"

I chuckled. "Your honesty is astounding. Let's try another question. Have you been seeing Peter since that time?"

"Yes. Whenever Peter came out here, we made it a point to get together." She seemed smart enough to realize that the email I had read could've been dated at any time over the last year.

"How often did he work with your company?"

"Not that often, but we'd get together whenever he came East, not just when he came to Philly. He made trips to New York, Washington DC, sometimes Baltimore. I'd go wherever he was if I could get away, or he'd come here when he finished with his business. Whenever we could work it out."

"Your husband never suspected anything?"

"No, he doesn't know anything. He travels a lot, so I have plenty of time on my own." It sounded like a familiar story. A big, lonely world. Spouses not happy in their current situation. And everybody left to their own devices. Poor babies.

"Did you see Peter on this latest trip?"

"Yes. I picked him up at the hotel on Friday and we spent the weekend at a cabin outside of Philadelphia that my husband and I own. I took him to the airport on Monday morning, dropped him off, and that's the last I've seen of him. I didn't know anything might be wrong until you emailed me." For the first time she seemed concerned, but whether it was for Peter or for the possibility of her involvement in his disappearance, I wasn't sure.

"No emails from him, or phone calls?"

"No, nothing."

"Have you tried to contact him since then?"

"No," she said. "Look, I'm almost home. Haven't I answered enough questions?"

"You don't seem very upset about all this."

"Hey, I'm no fool," her voice took on a cautious edge. "I enjoyed my time with Peter. We had a good time in bed, had some nice conversations, but that was all. He has his life and I have mine. If he's missing now, my first thought would be to see what other women are involved."

"Spoken like a true saint."

"Don't judge me, Mr. Ferguson. I'm trying to help you now," she said. "Please don't contact me again." The connection died.

I hung up and stared at the pictures of Peter. I still didn't know if one of the women was Sheila. Not that it mattered. It seemed Peter had a girl in every port. A little fun on the side, no strings attached. A wife at home who didn't say a word about it. "You must be really good," I said to his smiling image. "No wonder you look so smug."

I stood up and stretched, thinking about the conversation. I could now place Peter at the airport in Philadelphia on Monday. According to Detective Merrick, Peter hadn't taken his scheduled flight, or any other commercial flight, back to Denver. So where was he? The credit card transactions could help me narrow that. Had the police already checked this? Amanda could fill in some of these holes.

I glanced at the clock. Four-fifteen. Where was Miss Lonely-Hearts? Still at the club, more likely. As if an ESP connection had started, the phone rang again. I answered on the first ring.

"Reed, it's Amanda." She gasped, her breathing coming out in sharp spurts.

"Just the lady I wanted to talk to. Have you called the credit cards companies yet?"

"You've got to come out here! Right away!"

"Why?"

"I received a ransom note."

CHAPTER SIX

"We'll take this in for fingerprint analysis and let you know what we find out," Detective Jimmy Merrick said to Amanda. She stood in the middle of the room, rubbing her hands over her arms as if she couldn't get warm. "If you hear anything at all, call me right away."

I was standing in the Ghering's spacious living room, listening to Merrick, a tall, red-haired guy in wrinkled gray pants, white shirt and blue sport coat, his tie askew, wrapping up his interview with Amanda about the ransom note.

I had arrived just as the detectives were finishing. Merrick had the ransom note in a Ziploc bag, but he begrudgingly showed it to me after I showed him my driver's license, verifying who I said I was. He wasn't at all impressed with my presence, but Amanda made a scene about the police interfering with her right to hire an outside investigator. Merrick shrugged his shoulders, but offered little in the way of information. His partner, Randy Cash, had already gone.

"You want one last look?" Merrick said to me, holding up the baggy. Sarcasm dripped like sap at his offer.

"No, I think I've got it committed to memory," I said with just as much bite in my tone. If I couldn't remember the note, I should get out of the business, for it consisted of two lines. The first said, "One million - cash." The second, "We will be in touch." Printed on white paper, almost certainly done on a computer. Hardly anyone used a typewriter anymore. The note, paper, and print type were so common that I didn't expect any possible clues from it.

"Mrs. Ghering," Merrick nodded curtly to her and turned to leave, almost running into the massive Christmas tree.

"Thanks for your help," I said, acting on Amanda's behalf as Merrick sidestepped the tree on his way to the entryway. I felt like a butler escorting him out.

"Watch yourself."

"Excuse me?" I said.

Merrick held the door open, and he met my eyes with a cold gaze. "Watch yourself with her. She's not what she seems."

"How would you know?"

"Too many years on the job."

I searched his face, but nothing accompanied the warning. His face had the expression of a corpse. "Thanks for the tip," I said. Merrick stepped out into the cool night. I watched the detectives drive off in a white four-door sedan, then walked back into the living room and sat down.

"Now you see why I hired you," Amanda said as she slumped down into a leather chair across from me. She picked up a martini glass from a mahogany end table and swished the last droplets around, then tossed the drink back. With the other hand she twirled a curl of her hair, pulled it straight, then let it flop back onto her forehead. I had watched her do the same nervous motion while the detectives talked to her.

"They seemed competent," I said.

"Ha!" she spat at me. "They're not going to do anything. Pat the poor woman on the hand and leave." She managed her words carefully, in the way heavy drinkers do so no one knows they're drunk.

"They don't have much to go on," I said. I knew from our earlier phone call that upon returning from the country club, she'd discovered the note slipped partway under the doormat on the front porch. It had been folded in half, delivered without an envelope. She had called me right away.

"Does this mean that Peter's dead?" she asked, a hazy look on her face.

I stood up and walked over to her, taking her glass away. "I doubt it. In most cases, if the kidnappers ask for ransom, they keep the hostage alive so they can get the money. Kind of like leverage." I had no idea if this was true, but it sounded comforting. It seemed to work for her.

"I don't know what to do," she said, standing up. She grabbed the glass from me and walked a shaky path to a minibar at the far end of the room. She set the glass down with a clunk, poured Stolichnaya vodka into it, added a dash of vermouth, dropped a green olive in the concoction, and meandered back to her chair, sipping the drink as she went.

"Can you come up with that kind of money?"

"I don't know. I may have to involve his parents."

"They don't know anything?"

"Of course not. We don't talk to them much at all, the holidays mostly." She sucked the olive from the glass. While munching on it she said, "I didn't see any need to worry them, not when I didn't know what was going on."

"But you thought he was dead. That's seems like a good reason to involve them."

"Why tell them anything when I didn't know for sure? They'd be angrier at me for upsetting them needlessly if it all turned out okay." She tipped her head back and finished off the vodka. Her words were becoming more slurred. "You don't know Peter's parents. They're as insensitive as he is. Was. Oh man." She turned her head to the side and let out a sob, then recovered enough to head back to the minibar.

"What about your parents?"

"My parents certainly don't have that kind of money," she said as she mixed yet another martini.

"Do they know what's going on?"

She guzzled the drink down and said, "No, and I don't intend to tell them either. Not until this is resolved." She turned to face me, leaning against the bar for support. Anger and alcohol turned her face splotchy red. "If you must know, Peter and I don't have much contact with our families. They resented our getting married, and the rift begun then remains. That's the way they want it, so I haven't told them anything."

I watched her, contemplating this beautiful woman with a growing pity. Amanda Ghering, at the present moment, was a pathetic, drunken mess. I sighed as I watched her twirling her hair. I had a lot of questions about what was going on, but I decided against asking anything now. I stood up. "I don't know what we can accomplish at the moment. I'll call you tomorrow."

She turned her wet, mascara-smeared eyes to me. "Please, don't go. It's so lonely here." She reached a bejeweled hand out to me.

"I thought you didn't have affairs."

She smiled. "There's a first time for everything."

I was flattered, but as I looked into her hazy eyes, I knew that now was definitely not the time. I shook my head at her and left. As I opened the front door, I glanced back. She was walking back to the minibar, fixing another drink.

CHAPTER SEVEN

The next morning I slept late, ran some errands, and didn't get to the office until after lunch. And to my surprise, Amanda was pacing in the hall, waiting for my arrival. She looked like left-overs after a month in the fridge, wearing the same slacks and blouse from last night, the curl in her hair flattened, her eyes puffy and bloodshot, her face the color of ash. She was a walking hangover. And I didn't feel sorry for her.

"It's about time you got here," she fired at me. "What kind of detective are you?" She traipsed past me and tapped her foot while I unlocked the inner office door. Once inside, she eased down into the chair and said, "You have some explaining to do." I raised an eyebrow at her.

"I have some explaining to do?" I was prepared to confront her, but she was not following the plan I had in my mind. "What's going on here?"

"What did you tell the police last night?"

I sat back, staring at her. "I didn't tell the detectives anything. You did all the talking. Or don't you remember?"

"Don't be fresh with me," she clipped her words. "I know perfectly well what I said to them. Why wouldn't I?"

"Maybe because you were trying to crawl into a vodka bottle while they talked to you." I matched her intensity. "Do you mind telling me what this is all about?"

She slammed her purse down onto the floor beside the chair. Lipstick and a pocket mirror flew out of it. "I got a call this morning at eight o'clock. It was Detective Merrick. He'd like to ask me more questions about the note. If that would be okay."

"So?"

"So," she mimicked me. "He practically said that I wrote it, that I knew more about Peter's disappearance than I was telling them. He grilled me for half the morning." She pointed a finger at me. "You told them something to put the suspicion on me."

"Don't be ridiculous," I said. "I didn't talk to them at all. I was with you the whole time."

"You saw them to the door."

Apparently she hadn't been in a total blackout. Or her selective memory was better than I thought. "Where Detective Merrick warned me," I said. "About you."

"What do you mean?"

"He said, and I quote, 'things aren't always what they appear.'" I pointed at her. "That you might not be what you appear."

Her eyes became slits, warily contemplating me. "What does that mean?" she finally asked.

"You tell me. I know you lied to me."

"About what?"

"Now who's being fresh?" I said while she glared at me. "The plane ticket. Peter used his ticket from New York to Philly. And the police told you that."

"I must've made a mistake."

I didn't detect anything that made me think she was lying again. "Why are the police suspicious of you? Are you hiding something from them? From me?"

"The police always suspect the spouse. You should know that," she snapped.

"Would you like to start this conversation over?" I let Amanda think about that while I fixed her two of the most well-known hangover remedies known to man: coffee and water.

"Thank you." She accepted the coffee and ignored the water. I set the glass on a table beside the chair and went back to my desk.

"What aren't you telling me?" I asked, sitting down and crossing my arms.

She gulped the coffee. "Okay. The truth is, I knew about all the women."

"You told me that." My patience was slipping away.

"Yes, but I wanted to put some kind of suspicion on them. Whoever they were." The coffee seemed to be perking her up. "Peter ruined our marriage. I wanted the women to pay as well."

"Maybe they already had."

"I have no way of knowing that. I figured if I said that Peter didn't make it back to Denver, you'd have to go searching elsewhere to find him, and in the process, you'd have to bring these other women into the open. Expose the affairs to their husbands or boyfriends."

"But you had no way of knowing if these women were in relationships."

She shrugged her shoulders. "Some of them had to be."

I stared into her blue eyes, trying to find some feeling floating behind the hangover glare. Nothing but a cold stare. No emotion for her husband, certainly none for anyone with whom he was involved, or the unsuspecting partners.

"Tell me what the police told you," I said. "The first time you talked to them."

"Except for the thing about the plane tickets, I told you everything." She paused to sip more coffee. "The police didn't do anything. They filed a missing persons report. I gave them a picture of Peter and his itinerary, and they said a detective would look into it. After a day, Detective Merrick called me and said the plane ticket was used to Philadelphia, but not back to Denver. If Peter did fly back here, nobody knows about it. They did some checking at the airport, and with the airlines, but nobody specifically remembers Peter being on that flight, or any other."

Amanda's monologue was one helluva lot more than she had shared when I first met her. "What about the credit cards?" I asked. "Which ones did he use?"

She averted her eyes. "I haven't looked into it yet."

I shook my head slowly at her. "You sound an awful lot like someone who doesn't want to find her husband. Is there anything else you'd like to do to make this harder for me?"

"I am trying to help you," Amanda said, pouting. "You've got to believe me."

I stood up and came around the desk, handing her the phone. "Then call the credit card companies."

"Now?"

"Now." I held the receiver closer to her. She set the empty cup down and took the phone gingerly, as if it might shock her. "The numbers are on the back of the cards."

"You don't have to treat me like a child," she fumed, cradling the phone in her lap while she dug around for her wallet.

"Then quit acting like one."

I received a steely glare for that one. She selected five credit cards out of a deck. "These are the ones he carries. He uses the American Express for business. I have that card, but don't use it." I gestured to the phone. "All right. You don't have to get pushy." As she dialed a number she said, "This part of you I was not told about."

"Darn. I thought my charm was never-ending."

I watched her while she called the numbers, jotting notes on a pad I provided her. I read what she wrote after she completed the last call.

"He used AmEx on the seventh, paying for his hotel in Philadelphia," I said. That was a week ago, which meant that he'd spent the weekend with Sheila instead of returning to Denver.

"You didn't make the other charges?" I pointed out some charges on the list.

She shook her head. "No, I rarely use these cards."

"The Discover card was used at a gas station in Pennsylvania last Saturday," I said. "That could fit with what Sheila said. But why use the Discover card if he's got AmEx for business?"

Amanda's head jerked up and she grimaced. "When did you talk to Sheila?" There was poison in her voice. "What did she say?"

I smiled. "That's right. I haven't told you that." I sighed in an exaggerated manner. "I was going to tell you last night, but you didn't seem up for it."

"I was upset, okay? Stop harassing me about it."

"I talked with Sheila late yesterday afternoon. She told me about her and Peter, how they would meet on occasion, in Philadelphia, Baltimore, DC, or New York. Whenever and wherever it was convenient for them. She spent last weekend with Peter before dropping him off at the airport on Monday morning. That's the last she's seen or heard of him." I left out the part about appreciating Peter's sexual prowess.

"That jerk." Amanda sat back and chewed the inside of her cheek. She finally looked up at me and said, "You can see why I want her to suffer, too."

I shrugged my shoulders. "You're worried about Peter, but you still want Sheila to suffer?"

"Absolutely."

I shook my head, glancing at the poster of *The Big Sleep*. I'd found a dame right out of the movies: darkly seductive, and probably dangerous.

Amanda sat up straight in the chair. "What's the matter?"

"I'm wondering what I've gotten myself into."

"You're not giving up, are you?" Now she leaned forward on the edge of her chair, exposing some cleavage. "You can't do that."

"I never said I was quitting," I said. But as I contemplated her, I began questioning why I agreed to take the case in the first place, and more significantly, what my initial attraction to her was.

"Look, I need your help," Amanda pleaded. "I'll work with you, I promise. No more games."

I stared at her.

"Please," she said.

"No more games," I said.

She stared at me before nodding. "Would you like to go for a drink?" she said with a sudden switch in demeanor. She inched forward, trying to be sexy. She may have even batted her eyelashes, but my anger had returned, so I couldn't be sure.

"Amanda," I said, moving around my desk.

"Yes?" she asked in that seductive voice.

"Get out," I said. Without another word Amanda grabbed her purse, got up, smoothed her outfit, and flounced out the door.

CHAPTER EIGHT

I spent the rest of the afternoon trying to get some work done, but since there wasn't much of that to do, I finally left. I walked a few blocks over to B 52's, a converted warehouse that was now a pool hall decorated with old plane propellers and advertisements from a time long gone. I did a good bit of thinking there, shooting pool and letting my mind wander over whatever problem was at hand.

And Amanda was definitely a troubling, seductive problem. I cursed myself for not listening to my better judgment, and for letting her beauty pull me in. But whatever her goal was in hiring me, I had a sneaky suspicion that finding Peter was only part of the issue. And that bothered me. If she really didn't want him found, why hire me? It didn't make sense.

It was happy hour on a Friday, so the place was already getting crowded. I marched straight to the bar and ordered a Fat Tire. A busy bartender with his own tire-sized chest handed me a cold bottle of beer and I strolled to a pool table in the corner, racked up the balls, and began shooting while tunes from the 80's blared overhead. I felt right at home.

Two beers and six practice games later, I had determined only that I didn't trust my first client, and I was none too sure of my own instincts. Amanda smelled of more than expensive perfume, I thought, as I banked the cue ball off the side and behind the eight ball, hitting a striped ball into the corner pocket. On that brilliant, lucky shot, I left the game unfinished and headed home.

Since I live near downtown, I frequently walk to and from work. It makes for a good workout. That's what I tell myself on a dark night like this, one where the late winter temperatures hovered near freezing, and a light snow was falling.

I could see my breath as I scrunched up my shoulders, tucking my chin inside my coat collar. I walked at a brisk pace, headed toward my condo in the Uptown neighborhood, immediately east of downtown Denver. Christmas lights on houses and trees combined with the fresh snow to give everything a festive, holiday feel. The street, lined with parked cars on either side, was otherwise abandoned. The snow was starting to blanket the asphalt. I crossed diagonally toward my building, halfway down the block, and made my way between two cars to the sidewalk.

I dug in my pocket for my keys and stumbled on a crack in the sidewalk, falling to my knees. With a shake of my head I looked back toward the guilty piece of concrete that caused my fall. As I did, a shadow appeared out of the corner of my eye, coming from behind a wall of snow-covered hedges. I had just enough time to jerk in surprise before a shadowy specter materialized, its arm raised high in the night air. I noticed something dark and long, maybe a baseball bat, coming down toward me. I raised my arm in a feeble attempt to protect myself, heard a hollow thumping sound, and then a searing pain shot through my wrist. I groaned and grabbed my wrist with my other hand, and felt myself stumbling again.

"Stay away from Amanda," a low voice said. In an instant, I saw the club coming down toward my head, and everything went black.

————

"Wow, dude! What happened to you?"

I heard a moan, a curse word, then silence. I felt a hand on my shoulder, shaking me. I heard another groan and realized it was coming from me. I sensed cold underneath me and wet spots on my face. My encounter with the shadow came back in a sudden rush. I opened my eyes, and experienced something more terrible than my worst hangover.

The voice said, "Are you okay?"

My eyes focused and I saw shimmering gray clouds and snowflakes falling. If not for my cold backside and hangover-like headache, I might have appreciated its beauty. A face appeared above me, young with a stubble of dirty blond beard, eyes the same gray as the snowy sky. "Yeah, I'm okay," I mumbled. I sat up slowly and was rewarded with a pounding on the right side of my head.

"Dude, you're bleeding," the lazy, drawling voice said. I touched my temple and examined my fingers, now dark with blood. I forced my eyes to focus on the origin of the voice. Meet my neighbor Ace. I live in the third floor condo building and he and his brother live below me. Ace is twenty-five years old, works at Blockbuster, where he aspires to be a manager, and has the common sense of a pea.

"Your blood?" Ace asked, pointing at my hand. Make that a frozen pea.

I managed a nod while I wiped my fingers on the snowy sidewalk. "Yeah, someone popped me. Guess he got me pretty good." It hurt to talk, made the pounding in my head more intense.

"Popped ya, huh?" Ace bent down and squinted in my face, tugging at his ponytail. I could smell his tobacco breath, mixed with peppermint, and clouds of nausea swirled around me. "You don't look so hot."

"Thanks, Ace," I said. "You want to help me up?"

"Oh, sorry." He grabbed my outstretched hand and pulled me to my feet. Wooziness set in, like my head just split in two. I bent over and saw the snow shake before my eyes, so I sat back down on the ground. I heard another voice say, "What are you doing on the sidewalk? You want me to get you a chair?"

I turned my head and squinted toward the front door of my building, shielding my eyes against the glare of the porch light. Ace's brother, Deuce, stood in the doorway. He looked almost exactly like Ace, but with a bulkier build from working in construction. Deuce wasn't much younger than Ace, and by all accounts wasn't much wiser. "You want a chair?" he repeated slowly. "Maybe an icepack?"

Ace waved at him, and Deuce came down off the porch. The nausea hadn't left me, so I bent my head down between my knees and sucked in deep breaths, wishing that the Goofball Brothers would be quiet, if only for a moment. I kept an eye on them, and they did me. Sort of.

"He tired or something?" Deuce said as he approached. Most times I didn't mind the Brothers; we were friends in an intellectually unchallengeable kind of way. In the year that I'd lived above them they had helped me appreciate the lighter side of life, and made me laugh. Right now wasn't one of those times.

"Don't know," Ace answered. His drawl not as slow as Deuce's, a turtle rather than a caterpillar.

A pair of dingy tube socks and blue jeans came into my

vision. I tipped my head up and saw Deuce staring down at me. He wasn't wearing a shirt, and his bare arms folded across his brawny chest were his only defense against the weather. "Dang, it's cold out here," he said with a shiver, hunching his shoulders.

"Might help if you put shoes on," I mumbled. "And a shirt."

Deuce looked down at his stocking feet. "Oh, yeah." He chuckled. "What're you doing out here?"

"Someone popped me," I said, gingerly touching my temple again.

"Popped you?" Deuce said, glancing over at Ace, who shrugged his shoulders and made a face that said he didn't have a clue what was going on. "That guy with the baseball bat do it?"

"You saw him hit me?" I asked, gazing up at Deuce.

"Not hit you. He was getting into that SUV over there." We all looked down the street where Deuce pointed. Red taillights suddenly pierced the darkness, and a black, full-size SUV peeled away from the curb. Deuce started to run after it, but the vehicle disappeared into the night.

"He's gone," Ace stated the obvious.

"It had a broken taillight," Deuce said. "The left one."

I shook my head. "Help me up," I grimaced.

"I just tried to," Ace said. "You sat back down."

"I'll stay up this time. I promise." Ace grabbed my hand and yanked me to my feet, and this time I did stay standing. Wobbling and nauseous, but standing.

"You don't look so good," Ace said through chattering teeth.

"Is there an echo?" I asked no one in particular. It didn't matter. The brothers gawked at me in confusion. Like Two Stooges. Not too bright, but funny as hell.

Ace stooped down and picked something up. "Are these yours?" He held up my keys.

"Yeah, thanks," I mumbled.

"Hey, you want to come in for dinner?" Deuce asked. "Our brother's coming over."

"Who?" I asked.

"Dude," Ace rolled his eyes at me. "Our brother."

"What?" Now I was acting like a stooge. As far as I ever knew, there were only two Goofball brothers. "Another brother," I said. This was a night for surprises.

"Yeah," Deuce said. "There he is."

I was not ready for a third Goofball Brother. Not with my head pounding the way it was.

"Hey, what's going on here?" The voice was deep and sounded more assured than a Goofball Brother should.

I straightened up and put out an unsteady hand. There was no mistaking the man before me as a Goofball Brother. Although obviously older than the others, he had the same slim build and light hair, and the same stark gray eyes, but with wisdom lines flaring from the corners. I missed his hand on the first try. "Let me guess, you must be Trey."

"Huh?" he said, a not so bright look on his face.

Oh boy, this card didn't fall far from the pack. "If you're Trey, how can you be older than them?" I gestured toward the other two. "Shouldn't you be younger? You know. One," I pointed to Ace. "Two, three." I pointed at Deuce, then the new guy.

The man leaned closer to me, his eyes narrowing as he examined me. He sniffed near my face. "I can't smell any booze, so you're not drunk," he said. "But you look like maybe you're a few flames short of a fire."

I pointed to the blood near my temple. "Someone used my head as a baseball and took a bat to it. I'm a little woozy."

"Oh," he said with a sympathetic nod.

"Who are you?" I asked, not bothering to hide my own

confusion. I wasn't really close to the Brothers, but I thought I would've heard about another brother.

"I'm Bob Smith." He jerked his head toward his brothers. "I'm the oldest of the Smith clan."

"Bob," Deuce said. "Same forwards as backwards. Although he doesn't look the same from behind." Ace and Deuce snorted and guffawed at the joke, while Bob's left lip twitched up in an embarrassed smile.

"Dad hadn't discovered his love of poker until after I was born." Bob grinned. "That, or Mom wouldn't give in to the naming convention on the first kid." He took my elbow and propelled me up the steps and into the Brothers' condo. "Let's get a look at your head. I'm an EMT and I don't like the looks of you right now. It must've been one helluva whack to have you so out of it."

Now I had to reevaluate. The brains in the family must've come around only once, the first time. "An EMT? Do you work here in town?"

"Uh huh. Come on in here." Bob guided me to a couch in the living room. I laid my head back and closed my eyes.

"Here, get him a glass of water," Bob said. Ace mumbled something as he ambled to the kitchen at the back of the condo.

"Sit still." Bob ordered and I sat immobile while he carefully checked out the wound. "You've got a good-sized lump and a decent cut there, but it doesn't need stitches," he said. "That headache won't go away for a while, though." He dashed into the bathroom and returned with a First Aid kit. He took out butterfly bandages and proceeded to tape up the cut. I relaxed and almost dozed off.

"Are you feeling better?"

I opened my eyes again and nodded. Bob was sitting on a chair across from me, arms folded over his chest, smiling at me.

Behind his shoulder Deuce stared at me, still as confused as ever. Which reminded me. I sat up straighter, ignoring the ensuing throbbing, and studied Bob. "Why haven't I heard of you before? I've known your brothers for a year now."

"I don't know," Bob said. "I've heard of you."

I nodded, but was speechless.

"Deuce, why don't you help Ace with the pasta."

"Huh?" Deuce turned his stare to Bob.

Bob raised an eyebrow at him. "When you called me earlier, you said you guys were fixing pasta for dinner."

"Oh yeah." Deuce shuffled off into the kitchen, where we soon heard the sounds of pots banging onto the counter, and then the start of an argument between Deuce and Ace.

"I guess Ace forgot your water," Bob said.

I waved a hand at him. "Forget it. I should be going anyway." But my behind still stayed glued to the couch, contemplating this newest brother. How could I have missed this? I must have been tuning out the Goofball Brothers whenever they had talked about Bob. My observation skills needed honing.

"I haven't lived in Denver long," Bob said as if he could hear my thoughts. "I lived on the East Coast until a few weeks ago."

"Oh." I paused. "I should be going," I said again, but this time I forced myself out of my seat. I stood, swaying a bit.

"Are you going to make it?"

"Yeah, I'm just upstairs." I shook Bob's hand. "Thanks again for the help."

He showed me to the door. I stepped onto the porch and walked its length to the left side of the building, where a wet, metal staircase led to the third floor entrance to my condo. Behind me I could hear Bob chuckling, probably wondering what kind of a goofball lived above his brothers.

CHAPTER NINE

When I let myself into my place, I tramped right to the kitchen for Advil. I tossed two in my mouth and washed them down with half a bottle of water, then stumbled into the living room and crashed on the couch. I awoke later to the sound of the phone softly ringing, its pulse barely loud enough to rouse me.

I grabbed the cordless off of the end table and held it to my ear. "Hello," I mumbled, my voice sounding like I was talking through cotton.

"Honey, is that you?"

"Mom?" I propped myself up on one elbow and squinted at the clock on the wall. Ten-fifteen. I'd been asleep for more than two hours.

"Honey, are you all right? Did you swallow a frog? You're not doing drugs, are you? I never did, not even smoking pot, even though it seemed like everyone else did. They say that when you smoke pot, your mouth gets all dry and you sound like, well, like you do." My mother had a way of launching into a topic like a preacher into a hell-and-brimstone sermon, full force and not taking a breath. "Reed, this is not how we raised you, to blow your money on drugs, ruining yourself. Get a good job, find a nice lady, and settle down. Out doing drugs. Why, the next thing you know, you'll be on the streets, and then where will you be?"

"On the streets," I said.

She sniffed. "You're not funny, dear."

"It's good to hear from you, Mother. How are things in Florida?"

"Everything's fine here, but don't change the subject. How are you, really?"

"I'm just tired. It was a long day and I fell asleep on the couch." Half the truth was better than the whole thing. No way could my mother handle the whole truth. Not when her son was falling down in the line of duty, and especially not when my duty involved a profession that she saw as "chasing those people around for money."

"I'm glad you're working hard, but you need to take better care of yourself, dear. Now, I wanted to let you know that your father and I made our flight reservations. We'll be coming to visit in two weeks." She rattled off the dates for their annual Christmas visit and I pretended like I was writing it all down.

"Now it's late, so I'll let you go," she said. "I love you, dear."

"I love you, too, Mother." I hung up the phone and promptly fell back asleep.

I awoke the next morning with a splitting headache and a tender spot on my temple where the butterfly bandages held the cut closed. I also knew I wanted to find out what had happened to Peter Ghering, and why I was the target of an attack. As I stood in the kitchen fixing a bagel and cream cheese, I thought through what last night's assailant said to me: "Stay away from Amanda." Someone was taking an interest in my investigation, someone who was either tailing me or knew where I lived. Or both. But why was I such a threat? I'd barely gotten started on this thing. Was it about this case, or something else? Why stay away from Amanda? And the biggest question: who attacked me?

It was Saturday, so I lingered over a long breakfast, showered, then reapplied bandages to the cut on my temple. After a half hour of contemplation over a cup of coffee, I decided that I would focus on the source of my anxiety: Amanda. If she was hiding something, I wanted to know what it was. I'd had a bad feeling about her from the start, but my focus had gone in another direction, to finding her husband, Peter. It was time to turn my attention to her.

It was now almost eleven. I took two more Advil for my headache, threw on a pair of jeans, a sweatshirt, and tennis shoes and headed out the door. I stopped by the office to check messages — none — and grabbed a sandwich from Jason's Deli across the street. A light snow fell, and temperatures hovered barely above freezing, so I drove with caution over slick roads to Castle Pines.

Once in Amanda's neighborhood, I parked where I could see the road that led down to her house. I opened a Coke and ate my Italian sub sandwich while I waited. The DJ on the 80's radio station gabbed over the end of a Cars' song, saying that it was heading into the noon hour, time for the top five songs from the last week of April, 1984. I kept my eye on the bend in the road. It wouldn't be long now.

As if I'd just looked into a crystal ball, Amanda's gray Lexus came into view. She barely looked toward my vehicle. She yielded for a second before tearing off down the road. She hadn't even noticed me, unless the whack to my head had left me more addled than I realized. I could surmise where she was going - to her country club.

Sure enough, I followed the Lexus back onto the highway and soon exited on Lincoln Avenue, where Amanda drove straight to the Lone Tree Golf Club. I knew the club, had golfed there a few times the previous summer. Advertised as a premier private country club, with an Arnold Palmer designed course, the club catered to the social elite of south Denver.

Amanda turned into the circle drive entrance of the Lone Tree, got out, and handed her keys to a young valet who had helped her out of the car. She said something that made him laugh, pulled her long fur overcoat around herself and walked into the building. I had a feeling I was in for a long wait, at least a couple of hours. I hunkered down in the car seat, where I could still see the front door, turned on the radio, and sipped my Coke. The DJ was announcing the number one song from 1984, by the Thompson Twins. Amanda would like that.

I tapped on the steering wheel, humming the song. It finished, and REM came on. I hummed through that and two more songs as I watched the valet park cars. I was just thinking that I needed to use the bathroom when the valet drove up with a gray Lexus. I sat up as Amanda came out the door. I checked my watch, already knowing that she couldn't have been inside for more than a half hour or so. At her speed that was only a couple of drinks. What was going on?

She tipped the valet and peeled out of the drive and around the lot. Okay, maybe she'd gotten three drinks in her. I barely had time to duck before she came out of the exit, almost directly across from where I'd parked. She drove back toward the highway. As I did a U-turn I hoped she didn't recognize my 4-Runner. What kind of an amateur was I not to even try and hide myself?

But if Amanda spotted me, she either didn't care or was

lousy at losing a tail. She kept a steady speed of ten miles an hour over the limit as she headed toward downtown Denver. We kept that pace for ten minutes and I wondered if she was going to my office. But we soon came to the Cherry Creek Mall, an upscale shopping center. It appeared that Amanda was throwing over drinking for shopping.

I parked and followed after her, hearing her heels click on the concrete as she walked through a parking garage to the Neiman-Marcus entrance.

I got to the door and cautiously peered through the glass but didn't see her. I stepped inside, hoping she wasn't lurking somewhere nearby. I didn't see her at all. I frantically scanned the racks of clothes and displays, cursing under my breath. Then I caught sight of her, going toward the perfume and jewelry area. I started slowly down the aisle, prepared to peruse female lingerie while I kept my eye on her, but she moseyed right by the glass cases and out into the mall.

So, Neiman-Marcus wasn't her speed. I wondered what was. She walked at a fast clip past a bookstore and a couple of specialty shops. I could smell the tantalizing aroma of cinnamon rolls coming from the CinnaBun shop. Maybe she needed some dessert. My mouth watered. I could use some dessert.

But Amanda turned in another direction. I stopped and window-shopped at a shoe store while keeping my eye on her. She made a beeline to a triangular-shaped kiosk with a map of the mall on one side, an advertisement on another, and a pay phone on the third. Now I was puzzled. What was going on here? Surely she had a cell phone. Why use a pay phone? I could think of only two reasons: her cell phone battery was dead, or she didn't want any record that she made the call. If the latter, why?

She dialed a number, hung up, and dialed again. She spoke a

couple of words, then hung up. I watched her rummage in her purse, pull out a piece of paper, and dial another number from it. She turned in my direction, and I pulled back into the store entrance, glancing discreetly around the corner. Amanda was tapping her foot, apparently listening to endless rings on the other end. She hung up again, this time smacking the phone down harder, making a passerby glance at her. Amanda glared at the lady, threw the piece of paper back in her purse, and stormed back in my direction. I turned quickly and began inspecting a pair of red high heel shoes. Out of the corner of my eye Amanda passed by, looking straight ahead.

"Are you interested in those?" a young salesman asked me.

"Not my color," I said, setting the shoe down. He turned as red as the shoe while I hurried after Amanda.

She walked back through Neiman-Marcus, apparently heading straight for her car. I chose to leave her to her own business and ran back to the pay phone, just beating a teenage girl with enough gold on her wrists and fingers to stock a jewelry store.

"Excuse me. Emergency," I mumbled as I picked up the receiver that Amanda was using moments before.

The girl swore at me and walked off.

"Once a day and twice on Sundays," I said, with a curt nod. She looked fiercely at me.

I looked for a redial button, but there wasn't one. Obviously, I thought, not on a pay phone.

I swore and received a glare from an elderly lady who could've added diamonds to the teenager's jewelry store. I smiled at her and walked off.

So I hadn't found out who Amanda called, and now I didn't know where she was. Great.

CHAPTER TEN

A calculated guess took me back to Lone Tree, where I found Amanda's car, parked in a space close to the building. After a couple of hours, I was rewarded with only sore muscles and an intense case of boredom. I left her car there and spent the rest of my evening shooting pool with the Goofball Brothers.

I followed Amanda back to the club on Sunday, where she stayed for the entire day. Monday morning found me again parked near her house, hoping this time for a day more exciting than the daily sabbatical to the country club.

A storm front moving over the mountains made it colder, and the forecast called for more snow. I waited with the engine running, hoping nosy neighbors wouldn't notice me. At twelve o'clock on the nose Amanda's Lexus came into view. She seemed to be a creature of habit. I followed her to the club, dreading another day sitting in the 4-Runner. But after a few bored, slow hours, Amanda finally emerged, retrieved her car, and drove off.

The Lexus barreled onto I-25 and continued north. I barely had time to wonder where Amanda was headed before she turned into a gas station, the kind that also had a convenience store with it. She parked near the entrance and dashed inside, returning a few minutes later with a magazine. She got back in her car and drove out of the lot, with me still tagging along.

I puzzled over this development as I followed the Lexus to the Washington Park neighborhood, known for expensive homes near a spacious park. Amanda drove around a couple of blocks, to a posh little Italian restaurant on Clarkson Street called Patini's.

I parked across and down the street from her, and watched as she left her car near the restaurant and went in, the magazine rolled up in her hand. It was early, just after five, but it looked like the restaurant already had quite a crowd, especially for a Monday evening. I got out, crossed the street, and walked by the front window. I could see her through the glass, smiling in a cute way to a twenty-something looking waiter as he showed her to a two-seater table near the bar. She sat down, and I saw that she was carrying a comic book, not a magazine. She placed it in the middle of the table.

I looked on as she ordered not only a meal, but two drinks as well, chatting with the waiter each time he came to the table. He was tall and thin, wearing tight black jeans with a spotless white apron tied around his waist. But his rear end was at her eye level, so each time he walked away, she paid attention to it. Her husband didn't seem to be on her mind right now, but then he really hadn't been all along.

The bill finally arrived, and she paid with a credit card. After she signed the receipt, she took one copy for herself, turned the other over and wrote something on it, then got up and pulled on her coat. She lifted a hand in a coy wave at her waiter and walked out. The waiter waved back at her, came to the table and took the receipt, immediately reading the message on it. Amanda came out the door. I turned toward the window, staring at the waiter inside, with my back toward Amanda. An elderly couple seated by the window stared back at me in surprise. I ignored them as I waited for Amanda to discover me. But she walked quickly to her car, not noticing me in the darkness. Meanwhile the waiter tucked the receipt in his white apron pocket, picked up the comic, and headed for the kitchen. I was vaguely aware of the Lexus pulling out into the street as I dashed around the north corner of the building, looking for a back entrance to the restaurant. Amanda had passed that waiter a note, and I was going to find out what was on it.

I found the back entrance that led into the kitchen and stepped through an unlocked screen door. Even though the outside temperature was dropping, I could feel heat emanating from the hot ovens inside. I looked around until I saw Amanda's waiter, leaning his hands against a long metal prep table, waiting for an order of food to be filled. The comic stuck out of the back pocket of his black slacks. And no, I was not looking at his butt.

I made eye contact with him and gestured for him to come over.

He gave me a quizzical look, but walked over. "Who are you?" he said with a touch of surprise and a lot of annoyance.

"Archie Goodman," I said, flipping open my wallet to give him a nanosecond glimpse of my detective badge. "I'm a detective with the Denver Police Department and I need a word with you." If he asked to scrutinize the badge, I was in trouble.

"What's going on?" Not scared, just irritated. And not interested in verifying my credentials.

"Would you come with me, please?" He hesitated for a second before walking past me, tapping an older man on the shoulder as he passed by. "I'm taking a quick break," he said. The other guy rolled his eyes but said nothing.

We stepped outside and away from the small square of light that came from the kitchen door. He reached under his apron and pulled out a pack of cigarettes. A smoking break was probably a common occurrence, which was why no one stopped us.

He lit one, blew smoke into the crisp air, and contemplated me. "What's this about?"

"What did Amanda tell you?"

"Who?" he asked with genuine ignorance. A gold name tag pinned to his white shirt had "Jack" written on it.

"Amanda Ghering. The lady you served. The one who dined alone. She just left, and she wrote something to you on the receipt. What was it? What did she tell you?"

"Hey, screw you, man." He flicked the cigarette into a puddle of icy water, and tried to step around me. "I don't have to tell you anything."

I pushed him back against the brick wall, so fast that he exhaled with an "oomph" sound. For the first time, I saw fear in his eyes. "Now, you tell me what I want to know, or I'll haul your butt downtown and we'll talk there." I tapped him emphatically on the chest. "Your choice, Jack." Wouldn't the Denver Police be surprised when we showed up.

"Hey, all she did was leave her phone number on it, okay?" He stuck a hand in his pocket and pulled out a crumpled piece of paper. I grabbed it from him and examined it in the light from the kitchen. In Amanda's loopy writing, she had scribbled her name and phone number. Underneath that, she had written: "call me." I turned it over, but there were only the itemized menu items and totals for her meal and drinks.

"That's it?" I said with a stern glare.

"Yeah, that's it."

"Has she ever come in here before?"

He nodded. "A couple of other times, a few months ago.

She's a hot chick, okay. She's making her move, I'm making mine, you know?"

"All you've done is flirt with her?"

"She flirted with me," he corrected me. "That's not breaking the law." He squared his shoulders and pushed his way past me, saying, "what the hell kind of wacko cop are you?" Before I could respond, he disappeared back into the kitchen. I stood in the cold for a moment, puzzled and a bit embarrassed. Amanda was flirting with him. That could explain coming to this particular restaurant instead of the club, or a place farther south.

I shook my head and strolled back around to the front of the restaurant, still deep in thought. I glanced in the window. Jack was back at work, delivering drinks to one table, taking orders from another. I was about to walk away when I saw him reach behind him and take the comic book out of his pocket, dropping it onto a booth table near the exit. He picked up the bill from the table and walked away.

A slender hand came out and picked up the comic, then a tall brunette in a dark business suit and equally dark overcoat scooted out of the booth. The woman tucked the comic in her overcoat pocket, slung a small purse over her shoulder, and strode three steps to the exit. It all happened so fast that I didn't see her face at all. As she came out the door, I ducked around the corner and peered out. She hurried quickly down the street in the opposite direction of my car. I hesitated briefly, considered going for my car, thought better of it, and rushed after her. I tucked my head down into my coat, pulling up the collar, and walked with my eyes down. Dark Suit walked down one block and got into a black Chevrolet sedan. I was a half block behind her, so I stepped up my pace. I got a quick look at the license plate before the car squealed away.

I said it repeatedly so I'd remember it as I passed back by the restaurant, and around the corner. I jerked open the kitchen door, walked past a surprised cook and waitress, and up to Jack, who had just come in from the front. He opened his mouth in surprise and started to head back through a swinging door to the restaurant, but I grabbed his arm and pedaled him right on through the prep food tables and ovens. He sputtered in protest as I threw him out the back door. He stumbled into a big plastic trashcan, and fell to one knee.

"What the hell are you doing?" he snarled, picking himself up.

"That's what I want to know," I snarled right back. I grabbed him just as he was regaining his balance, and threw him into the wall. "Hey," he said.

"What's going on with the comic book?" I asked, pinning him face first against the wall.

"Wha..." he mumbled.

"I saw you pass the comic book to Ms. Dark Suit," I said, my face an inch from his cheek, my teeth bared. "You passed the comic from Amanda to her. Why?"

"What?" he said, his voice shaking.

"I won't ask again." I tightened my grip on his arms, nearly lifting him off the ground.

"Okay, all right." He coughed. "They paid me."

"Who?"

"I don't know her name. The lady in the dark suit." The confession came fast. "She came in one day a few months ago, said that I could make an easy hundred every time I'd make a delivery for her."

"Deliver what?"

"Comics, man. That's it. She said someone might come in, request to sit at my table, and leave a comic for me. She said to hang on to it, that someone would be in afterward to get it."

"What kind of crap is that?"

"It's the truth, I swear," he said, struggling against me. "Hey man, let go. I swear that's it."

"How many times has this happened?" I asked, loosening my grip slightly.

"Three times. Twice before tonight. It was the same two ladies. The pretty one, Amanda, ate and left a comic book, two times. I passed it to the other lady, and she left an extra hundred with her bill."

"A comic book?" I repeated.

"Yeah, a Spiderman comic. One other time the lady in the dark suit left a comic with a hundred in it. It was an X Men comic that time. I took the hundred and left the comic for that lady Amanda. That's it, I'm telling you. Leave me alone, man. I'm going to be in a boatload of trouble with my boss if I don't get back."

"You're going to be in boatload of trouble if you're lying to me." I pressed him into the wall for good measure.

"It's the truth." We were both breathing heavily as I released him. He turned around, rubbing his wrists where I'd held him. He slid along the wall to the back door. "You're crazy, man. Crazy."

"And you better hope I believe you," I said. He looked at me with near terror. It took him two attempts before he got the screen door open. Then he disappeared inside. I almost laughed at his fright.

CHAPTER ELEVEN

It was time to talk to Amanda again. I'd made that decision before walking out of the alley, so Tuesday morning I was parked in Amanda's driveway at exactly nine o'clock. I had a suspicion, based on my own experiences with too much alcohol, that she would still be in bed, and I was right.

"Too much vodka last night?" I said when she answered the door, bleary-eyed and tired, after the fourth ring.

"Reed," she said, her voice a gravelly mix of cigarettes and semi-sleep. "I was hoping you'd stop by." She wore a stark white terrycloth robe open to her navel. The silk nightgown underneath was too sheer for the cold weather, accentuating body parts I didn't want to know about. I focused on her face, ashen from what I'd guess to be a massive hangover.

"We need to talk." I pushed past her and into the living room.

"What's the matter," she asked, shutting the door. "Aren't you still looking for Peter?"

"Yes, I am. But I want to know what's really going on." I stalked to the bar and leaned against it. She'd have to step through me to get to any liquor. I crossed my arms and inspected her. She had dark circles under her eyes, and the white robe drained her face of any color. To say she looked like a ghost would be an insult to Casper and his relatives.

"What do you mean?" She held a hand to her ear, as if our voices were a cacophony of out-of-tune instruments, while she eyed the bar behind me. I'm sure the vodka was calling to her.

"You've had me on a wild goose chase, haven't you?" She didn't answer. "I've been running around trying to figure out where Peter is, but he's dead, isn't he? You had him killed, just like you said. You hired someone to kill him, and now you're trying to cover your tracks by making it look as if you're concerned. Then you hired me, and you've had me calling around to credit card companies and checking with the police. Merrick probably tracked all of that down, but you made me do it again, to keep me busy, and misdirected. And you made a fake ransom note. 'We will be in touch.' Like *any* ransom note would say that." I couldn't keep the derision from my voice. "What other crap have you concocted?"

"No, that's not it." She waved her hands nervously. "You don't understand."

"Obviously," I retorted as she shook her head vigorously, then blanched from the effort.

"Level with me, or I'm out of here right now," I said.

"No, please," she pleaded, clasping her hands as if in prayer. "You're right. I haven't been honest with you." A long pause stretched out before us, but I wasn't going to rescue her. She could fall into the proverbial hole she'd made. She finally let out a huge sigh, and began. "You're right," she said again. "I did hire a group to take care of Peter, but something happened. They were supposed to kill him before he ever reached Philadelphia, but they didn't."

"How do you know?" I still didn't trust anything Amanda said.

"Because Peter contacted me after the time he was supposed to be dead." I didn't have any response to that. "I was sort of telling the truth when I hired you. I did want you to find him, to find out why he *wasn't* dead. But I couldn't very well tell you that."

"But why me?"

She sighed. "I heard about you from someone at the club."

"Sure," I said. "I've built up such a reputation for myself."

"No, really. Paul Burrows knew your father's friend and knew how you helped him. I thought you'd be perfect. You'd only helped that one guy, you were brand new, hadn't really done much detective work."

"I'm inexperienced," I translated.

"Yes." She threw her hands up. "For crying out loud, I didn't think you'd actually figure any of this out."

I bit my tongue, cutting off a snide reply. "Did you lie about the plane ticket, and not helping the police with the credit card information?"

"Yes."

I let out a long breath. "If you want Peter found, why send me in the wrong direction?"

"If you weren't sure where Peter was, maybe you'd contact some of his lovers. Then they'd suffer for what they've done to me."

I glared at her.

"I was going to tell you about the ticket. And about the credit cards," she said sourly.

"So what's all this business about passing comics books at Patini's?"

Her jaw dropped. "You've been following me?"

"Surprise," I said. "I've figured out a lot. I knew something wasn't right almost from the start. I just didn't know what. You've never seemed that concerned about Peter, and that made me wonder about you. What you might be up to."

She thought about that before she responded. "But it wasn't just about finding out what happened to Peter. There's more." I waited. "I think the group is after me now."

"How do you know?"

"I'm being followed," she said.

"Was it a 4-Runner? Gray?" She nodded her head. I tried not to smile. "That was me." She turned red. "I thought that was them," she said, but with no relief.

"It's okay. I've been tailing you for two days. And by the way, what's with making phone calls from pay phones at the Cherry Creek Mall? Why not from somewhere around here?"

Amanda blushed. "I thought if the call was somehow traced, it would be better if the call was placed far away from my house."

I rolled my eyes at her illogical logic. "Why are you worried about calls being traced?"

"Oh, it doesn't matter! They're still after me." She covered her face with her hands, muffling a sob.

"Who?"

"The people I hired," Amanda said. She finally worked around me and reached for a glass.

"How about doing this straight?" I said, grasping her wrist.

"Just water, then." Her hand shook as she filled a glass with water and sat on the sofa. After draining half the glass, she repeated, "I think the group I hired to kill Peter is after me now. I, uh, wasn't exactly truthful with them."

"Are you with anybody?"

She threw a vicious look at me. "I made it sound like Peter was a monster. That way this group would take care of him for me."

"Why?"

"I wanted him dead," she stated flatly. "I wanted the money, not him. Our marriage was... is... nothing anymore."

I locked eyes with her, staring her down. "No, there's more than that. You're not fooling me."

She held my gaze for at least ten seconds before averting her eyes. "All right." She threw up her hands. "I was afraid Peter was going to divorce me. He didn't care anymore, he wasn't trying to hide his affairs, and he'd been dropping hints about a separation. I didn't want to go back to having nothing. So I hired this group. But now," she whispered, "but now, I wish I hadn't done any of this. I want Peter back. Not because I love him. I don't. I made a mistake. But if I can get him back, we might be able to work something out."

I heard voices in my head, one saying *I told you so*, the other, *you should've dropped this case when you had the chance*. I ignored them. "You need to see the police."

"No!" she said. "If I go to them, I'll be dead within days. This group does not play around. They made that very clear." I saw the fear leap into her face, and I had no doubt what she said was true. Whoever she hired would not risk exposure of any kind. "I need your help."

"What good is finding Peter going to do? He'll divorce you for sure."

"Not if I can convince him not to. And that doesn't really matter now, anyway. But if we find Peter, we can expose the group. They made a mistake keeping him alive, and I can use that against them." She was arguing for her own life, as well as Peter's.

"And Peter will be grateful to you in the end, and not leave you penniless." The spark in her eyes told me that even fear of death didn't keep her from thinking about money. "That's pretty shaky," I said.

"It's all I have."

I sat down on the other couch and regarded her. She was a scared, lying, conspiring woman. But could I walk away knowing what I did? Could I let harm come to her, and not feel terrible, even if she'd brought all this misery on herself? Didn't that lower me to her level? And could I rest not knowing where Peter was, or what happened to him?

"Who is this group?" I asked, grabbing the rope that would pull me further in.

Immense relief flushed over her face. "I don't know anything about them. They're an underground group that goes by the name X Women. I found out about them from a friend at the club."

"Is it that common to get rid of your spouse, that you can just get a name from someone at the club?" I spoke in a mock imitation of a snooty rich person.

"Don't be coy," Amanda said.

"Who told you about them?"

"I can't…"

I held up a hand to stop her protests. "Tell me. If you want to get to the bottom of this, you'd better."

"But she'll kill me," Amanda used the expression without thinking.

"And if she doesn't, this underground group will."

She paled, then blurted, "Maggie Delacroix. She gave me a number. She didn't even write it down, she made me memorize it. And before you ask, I have no idea how she knows of them, or if she ever used them."

"Is she a friend of yours?"

"Not really. I see her around the club."

"What do you know about her?"

Amanda waved a hand at me, like she was shooing a fly away. "What does it matter what I know about her? She's just some lady at the club. She's married to some rich guy who owns paper warehouses or something. He's her second husband. I think she's got kids, a daughter or something. I don't know Reed."

"Okay," I said, trying to calm her down. "So you contacted this group, and then what?"

"The person who answered told me to go to Patini's with a Spiderman comic and leave it with a waiter named Jack."

"I knew you didn't like Superman," I said.

Her eyes flashed at me and she bit off a protest, remembering that I had followed her. "Most of the contact was made through signals like that. It was a type of code. The only time I met face to face with anyone was after I left the comic the first time. I was contacted again, and told to go to Washington Park and wait near the boat rental place. A lady met me there, and I told her what I wanted. We spoke for about five minutes. I was supposed to return to Patini's in a week. If they accepted, Jack would pass me an X-Men comic. If nothing was passed, they had declined to take me on as a client."

It all sounded so professional, as if it was a mundane business transaction, not a death deal. "So they accepted. What happened next?"

"I got a call and was instructed to wire five hundred thousand dollars to an account in the Cayman Islands. They'd take care of everything from there." So that was the going rate. Pathetic.

"Where did you get that kind of money?"

She rolled her eyes at me. "Please, we have that in our accounts. I can access it just as easily as Peter."

"He didn't notice?"

"I lied to him. I said that our accountant suggested we transfer some of the money into a new bank."

"He didn't find that suspicious?"

"No. I handle some of our finances, and he's too busy to pay a lot of attention to the details."

"Okay. Who did you wire the money to?"

She shrugged her shoulders. "I don't know. The caller gave me an account number to wire the money to. That's what I did."

"Do you still have the account number?"

"Sure," she said. Her purse was sitting on the floor in the hallway. She got it, rummaged around and pulled out a piece of paper. She handed it to me. It had the account number, the name of a bank, and also a phone number.

"This is the number you called to get in touch with this group?" She nodded. "Didn't Maggie make you memorize it?"

She blushed. "I was afraid I'd forget it," she said sheepishly. "It's useless now. It's disconnected. When I called it the other day, the woman said the number wouldn't work anymore, and I was to wait for them to contact me."

I sighed. The plot thickened. "So after you paid the money, you didn't have to help set up Peter?"

"They do all of that," she said. "Someone called me one more time, gave me the time frame for the deal, and told me what to do when Peter didn't come home. That was it. I wasn't supposed to contact the group again. Ever. No matter what happened. If something went wrong, they would contact me."

"You were supposed to go to the police, report Peter missing, and leave it at that."

She nodded.

"But you didn't leave it at that."

She protested. "I did it according to plan. They gave me a date, last Monday, but not where or how. Just the date. I went to the police after a few days, when I thought it would make sense. I had to take Peter's normal behavior into account," she said like she was talking to a child. "But since Peter called I've been in a panic. So I decided to come to you."

"And now, since you've breached the group's code of conduct, you think they're after you."

Her lower lip trembled. "Yes," she whispered. "Now they'll come after me. I don't know what to do."

"Is this why you've been passing comics again?"

"Yes," she said. "They wouldn't do that if everything was okay. They asked for me to be available to them, that the plan had changed. Passing the comic was my answer."

"Which was?"

"Yes," she spat. "I don't have much choice, do I?"

I nodded. "They're not happy with you, are they?"

CHAPTER TWELVE

"I'm looking for Maggie Delacroix," I said to the pert receptionist at the country club. "She said she'd meet me in the bar."

I had convinced Amanda that I had to contact Maggie in
order to track down the group she hired. Once she'd had a
drink, she called Maggie and dropped the news that someone
else knew about their contact with the group. Maggie resisted,
but Amanda pleaded, begged and finally pointed out that I
would find Maggie anyway, so she might as well get the meeting
out of the way. I was wary of the compliment, even as Amanda
arranged to have me meet Maggie at the club. I left Amanda to
her second drink of the morning and drove to the country club.

"Yes, she informed me that she would have a visitor. Down
the hall on your right."

I retraced my steps from the other day and entered the bar.
Amanda had described Maggie as an elderly woman, with gray
hair and too many wrinkles to be attractive anymore. I was
instructed to look for her at a table by the windows that faced
west. As I stepped into the bar, I immediately noticed Maggie,
but not because the description fit. Just the opposite.

Maggie was edging toward sixty, with dark hair dramatically streaked with light gray. As she looked up at me, I noticed hints of wrinkles at the corners of her eyes, but otherwise her face was plastic-surgery flawless. She wore an understated blue pantsuit, had a large diamond ring on her left fourth finger, and smelled subtly of expensive perfume. My only criticism would be a bit too much makeup. Reflecting on Amanda's description, I'd say she was jealous of Maggie, and I could see why. Amanda's drinking would age her at twice the pace of someone like Maggie.

I sat in the chair Maggie indicated. "I don't think introductions are needed," she said, pushing the remains of a salad bowl off to the side of her place mat. She lifted a glass of water to her lips, took a tiny sip and said, "I really don't know that I can be of any help to you." Maggie was trying to play it cool, but I noticed that her glass shook as it came back to the table.

"Let me make it clear that I have no intention of bringing you into any of this."

"You already have," she said.

I shrugged. A waiter came to the table but Maggie shooed him away. I wouldn't be staying long enough to finish a drink. "Amanda screwed things up and she's probably in danger."

"Amanda is a stupid woman," Maggie said through pursed lips. "I never should have recommended her."

I agreed with her, but continued. "I need to know how to find this group. I don't know or care what your involvement with them is. Tell me about them and I won't say a word about you."

"Impossible," Maggie said. "Even if I had that kind of information, I couldn't give it to you." I knew she couldn't either. Her life wouldn't be worth the ice in her glass if she did.

"How do you know of them?"

She leaned forward in her chair. "I found out the same way

Amanda did. By asking a question here and there, by presenting my need to the right people. By listening to rumors. There are ways to do anything, especially if you have the means."

"How did you contact them?"

"I can't tell you that."

"Did you pass comics back and forth?"

"I'm sure I don't know what you're talking about." I was sure she did. She wasn't that good a liar. She took another sip of water. "I have far too much to lose to tell you anything. Amanda was foolish to even mention me."

"I hate to make threats, but I can make things very uncomfortable for you if you don't help me."

The water glass stopped halfway to the table. "That is a threat." I nodded as the glass clinked to the table. "What would you do?"

"The police aren't doing much right now. I'm sure a phone call from me would at least bring them to your doorstep. At this point, no one knows we're having this conversation, and no one knows about your involvement, other than Amanda and me." I paused. "And whoever you had killed."

"I never hired them for myself," she snapped. "I did it for a friend." Her voice grew quiet. "A very close friend."

I threw up a hand. "You all make it sound so business-like," I said. "You're still implicated in this whole thing."

She didn't respond. I waited. She thought. "They are an organization referred to as the X Women," she finally said, speaking in a hushed tone. "They work for the rights of women. They take on cases where a woman has been abused, where rape has occurred, or domestic violence, that sort of thing. They seek justice when it doesn't occur within the boundaries of our ineffective legal system." A hint of emotion split the calm demeanor. "I can contact them in the same manner as Amanda. Through a phone call. I have never personally met anyone, nor have I hired them for my own revenge." She wanted that last point made very clear.

"How do you know of them?" I asked. "Amanda said the number she had would be disconnected by now."

"Did you try calling it?"

I shook my head. "Not yet. I wanted to do it where it couldn't be traced."

Her lips moved into the suggestion of a smile. "That's good. You're giving them the appropriate credit. They are not a group to be trifled with." A finger tapped the table. "And Amanda is correct about the number. It will be useless to you now."

"Then how could you get in touch with them when Amanda can't?"

"Amanda is a stupid woman," she repeated. "She has broken group protocol, so the organization will now take measures to ensure they are not compromised by that stupidity. For myself, I have my resources, but I will not reveal them to you." She sat back and crossed her arms defiantly. "I have nothing else to tell you."

I contemplated her. "An organization called the X Women, huh." Great, I was trying to find an outlaw women's group who carried out vigilante justice. PMS meets Marvel Comics. "I don't suppose I can find a listing for them on the Internet."

"You are not funny, Mr. Whatever-Your-Name-Is." She waved the bartender over and asked for her bill. As she signed it, she continued. "Whether you believe it or not, this organization does good work. There are people, usually men, I'm afraid, who do little more than clutter up this lovely planet we live on. This organization helps in some small way to rid the earth of vermin." She used a well-manicured hand to brush an errant curl off her forehead. "Our justice system leaves a lot to be desired. Murderers, rapists, sadists, abusers, too often get away with little or no retribution. This organization sees that, at least some of the time, this does not happen."

"I'm sure they're just grand." I couldn't hold back my sarcasm.

She strained to stay calm. "When my daughter was in high school, she was friends with a sweet young girl. This girl, I won't tell you her name, was around a lot. I got to know her. She had a good heart, was maybe a bit innocent, but that's never been a crime. She was around so much that she soon seemed like my own daughter. The two girls did everything together; they were inseparable. They even chose the same college so they could remain close." She paused for effect. "That wonderful girl was abducted, tortured, raped, and strangled to death one night coming home after a date. The police had a suspect, but he was an all-star on a prestigious, winning football team. Even though the police knew this young man was guilty, they had to answer to very influential people who could sway the balance of justice. No charges were ever brought against him. Nothing was ever done. We were all devastated, her parents especially. I wasn't willing to sit by idly, and I had the means to do something where her parents couldn't. I made inquiries, found out about this group, and contacted them. Soon after, the football player had an unfortunate accident that killed him. As I said, this group does good work. Justice was served."

I met her steady gaze. "I'm sorry about your daughter's friend, but justice was not served."

She got up. "You are entitled to your opinion. I expect never to see you again." She turned and left, her back stiff, her head held high, as if she balanced a law book on it.

CHAPTER THIRTEEN

I called Amanda and told her briefly about my meeting. Judging by her slurred words, she was well past drunk.

"Why don't you take it easy," I chided her.

"I have a lot of tension in my life right now," she said in excuse of her behavior.

"And your life is in danger," I countered. "You need to be able to think clearly."

"I'm thinking just fine, thank you," she said, acid in her voice.

I let that be. "Do you know the name of Maggie Delacroix's daughter? One who was a friend with a girl who was murdered?"

Amanda hissed into the phone before answering. "Janet." She didn't want to tell me, but she knew she had to.

"Do you know the friend's name? The girl who was murdered?"

"No," she said.

"Where did Janet go to college?"

"I don't know." Anger rose in her voice.

I hung up before I could hear her start to ramble about me

RENÉE PAWLISH

prying into areas I didn't need to. I drove to my office, checked
my messages, none of which needed my immediate attention,
and spent an hour tracking down the license plate of the car I'd
seen leave the restaurant last night. The sedan belonged to
Enterprise Car Rental, a dead end for me. I retrieved the mail,
which consisted of bills and a box of oranges, shipped fresh
from my parents. I took the box and headed up into the mountains west of Denver. Maggie, who said she didn't have any
information to share, had told me quite a bit. Now it was time
to call in some help.

"She sounds like quite a lady," said my friend, Cal Whitmore.
Cal is akin to Sherlock Holmes. He has more knowledge loaded
into his brains than the Smithsonian has items on display. The
guy seems to know every obscure thing there is to know about
everything. However, unlike Holmes, Cal has a hard time
finding his way out of the house. He's brilliant but has little
common sense.

I had finished relating everything that had happened since
I'd taken on Amanda as a client, and was sitting in Cal's office
cum computer room. The rest of his house was sparse, but his
computer room was cutting edge. Cal boasted things that probably weren't on the market, certainly stuff I wasn't familiar with,
nor did I know how to use. He had a hard drive filled with a
variety of musical genres that he listened to on state-of-the-art
speakers, and watched DVDs on one of his four computers, the
one with the thirty-inch screen. Stacks of papers, manuals, and
other assorted computer stuff were piled against one wall, and
boxes of disks, wire, CDs, and other accessories leaned against
another wall. I could write my name on the dust that covered
everything except the computers, and at any given time dishes,

cups, glasses, beer bottles, and soda cans littered the room. He owned the house, but the computer room was where Cal lived. "Maggie is a mystery in and of herself," I said, throwing Cal an orange from my parents.

He caught it deftly. "These are good ones, known for their sweetness." Cal tossed it from one hand to the other. "A Valencia orange."

I knew from the package the oranges came in that he was correct, but he hadn't seen the box. "How do you know that?" I shouldn't have been shocked, but I was. I've known Cal since grade school, and I've seen him deduce amazing things.

"It's pretty easy, really," Cal said in a matter-of-fact tone.

I nodded my head and waited for more.

He held the orange up to a small desk lamp, examining it. "See its color, the green blemishes, and how it seems kind of marked?" He pointed to a faint streak on the skin of the orange. "That's called wind-scarring. Comes from the Florida breezes. The warm temperatures cause chlorophyll to return to the peel, giving it the greenish color. The skin's thin, and," he gently squished the orange, "it's easy to squeeze."

"That's impressive," I said.

"Besides, your parents are in Florida, right?" I nodded my head. "This is the season for Valencias. It's too late for Hamlins or Navels." I stared at him. "I put all the information together," he said blandly in answer to my awe. He looked closely at the orange, then squeezed it again. "It's ripe."

"Mom thought I'd enjoy them," I said. "She says 'hi', by the way." Mom has a soft spot for Cal, ever since I brought him home one afternoon after school, crying from a bee sting he'd suffered when he put his face right up to a furiously buzzing hive.

"Tell her I said 'hey'." He smiled. "Anyway, the season for Valencias is ending, but you can still get some good ones." Cal bit into the peel and grimaced. No common sense. I shook my head as he spat out the rind. I had a hard time envisioning Holmes doing that.

"Even if the skin is thin, it helps if you peel it," I said, taking the fruit from him. I peeled the rind off and handed back a juicy section, keeping some for myself.

"So what do you need me to help with?" Cal asked as he turned back to his computer, not fazed by his mishap with the orange. Cal's specialty was computer viruses and virus protection. He was more than his own business, he was like a computer god. Cal was involved with people and groups that I didn't even want to know about. He could hack into almost any system, even the Pentagon's. Cal was a recluse, lived on the fringes of the law, and rarely ventured anywhere. He almost didn't exist, and if he wanted to, he could make himself disappear.

"I have the license plate number of the woman Amanda passed the comic to." I flopped on an ancient love seat across from him, throwing my legs over the arm and letting my feet dangle. "It belongs to Enterprise Car Rental." I waved clouds of dust away from my face.

"I'm listening." He typed on the keyboard while talking. "Who played Ole Andersen in the 1956 film *The Killers?*"

"Burt Lancaster," I said through another bite of orange. "I highly doubt an organization like this would use real names, or credit cards, so I'm not going to waste anymore time with that. But if I could follow the money trail, it would eventually have to lead to some real person who wants access to the money." Cal nodded. "Is that something you could help with?"

"Sure, that's easy," Cal said, running a hand through his wavy brown hair. "What information did Amanda give you?"

"I've got the account number that she wired the money to, and the name of the bank in the Cayman Islands."

Cal laughed. "That sounds like something out of a movie. *Wire it to my account in the Caymans*," he spoke in a scratchy, quiet, Marlon Brando voice.

"Tell me about it," I said. I threw a piece of peel at the back of his head. It sailed by his right ear and landed by the computer speaker. He didn't even notice. "Have you ever heard of an organization of women called the X Women?"

He wagged his head back and forth in a negative response. "Who wrote, directed, and starred in *Touch of Evil?*"

"Orson Welles. How do you find out about a group like that?" I situated myself more comfortably on the couch. "These women act like it's no big deal to be asking around and then being told about a group that kills people. You should've seen Maggie and Amanda. They talk as if they're trying to find someone to help them invest their money."

Cal stopped typing. "What was the name of the group?"

"The X Women."

Cal connected to the Internet, and typed "X Women" into the search line. I could see a list of web sites appear on the screen.

"Whoa, should've known that would happen," Cal said.

"What?" I didn't have the energy to get off the couch.

"The X Women. Anything with 'X' in it is bound to bring up some porn sites." He scrolled through the list. "Here's one for a women's water polo event. Doubt that's it." He clicked and went to the next screen. "No, not there." He scanned through more of the results, periodically clicking on a site. He read off some of the names, but none of them had anything to do with an underground group of any kind, or killers for hire, not that either of us thought we would find a web site. "I'll spend some time looking into that." Cal said. "There might be something on the hack sites."

I nodded, contemplating the designs on his ceiling. "This is what I'm wondering. They have to be organized somehow, and have connections, and that sort of thing, right? If wealthy women can find out about them, we should be able to."

"They can't exactly advertise in the Yellow Pages."

"Duh," I said. "But I'm a detective; I should be able to find them, right?" Cal shrugged. "Thanks for the vote of confidence."

He was smiling, I could tell. "What is considered the first *film noir* film?"

"*The Maltese Falcon*. It's a great movie," I said.

"Who directed it?"

"John Huston. It was his directorial debut." I sat up. "What're you doing?"

Cal tapped the computer screen. "A detective *film noir* crossword puzzle."

"Oh." Cal may know a lot, but I was the old-movie buff, especially old detective movies. I moved over to the computer and looked over his shoulder. He had the puzzle almost completed, which showed he knew almost as much as me in this area.

"You'd better be careful," Cal said. "If Amanda had anything to do with Peter's death, she could be capable of anything, too."

"I hear you." I pointed to the screen. "That's *D.O.A.*"

Cal typed in the answer. "Dennis Quaid and Meg Ryan starred in a remake of an original movie starring Edmund O'Brien? I didn't know that."

I laughed. Rare words from Cal.

———

I left Cal's house around midnight. He had his assignment. He was going to follow the money trail, and he would find out anything he could on the X Women. I didn't know how much time I had with any of this. The X Women wanted something from Amanda, and I didn't think they'd wait to get it. On top of that, I also needed to figure out what happened to Peter Ghering. Was Amanda telling the truth? She appeared to be, so that brought up another question: where was Peter? And why did the X Women spare his life?

I mulled over the conversation with Cal as I made the journey back to downtown Denver. Cal lived in the foothills west of Denver, off of Highway 285 past the mountain community of Pine Junction. I followed a winding dirt road to 285, turned left and on to 285, and drove in the moonlight back to Denver. I was alone on the road, but still sped cautiously over the winding road, slowing as I rounded a sharp bend. When I came out of the curve, a full-size SUV pulled in behind my 4-Runner. Despite its bulk, the SUV quickly gained speed behind me. I accelerated until I was going ten over the speed limit, but the driver of the SUV kept pace with me. I glanced uneasily in my rear view mirror as the SUV headlights inched closer and closer toward the rear end of my vehicle. I picked up more speed, but the SUV stayed right on my tail.

"Okay, I'm going," I muttered, watching my speed top seventy as I veered around a sharp turn. The road dropped off a few feet on the right, the direction where the momentum of the turn was pulling me. I felt the left wheels of the 4-Runner lose grip with the road for a second, then regain traction. The SUV matched my speed as we roared around another bend. The road straightened. I sped up, the speedometer going over eighty, but the headlights glared right in my rear-view mirror. I looked for a pullout, a wider spot on the road that allowed slower cars to pull over and let others pass, but I saw none.

"Get off my butt," I muttered.

I gripped the wheel tighter as we rounded another dangerous turn and hit the brakes, slowing down. The SUV headlights disappeared from the mirror. I braced for a hit, unconsciously hitting the gas. The 4-Runner leaped forward, coming within inches of the guardrail on the right. I caught a brief glimpse of blackness dropping off into space before I eased up on the pedal. My tires screamed, but kept their purchase on the pavement. I raced around three more bends with the SUV on my tail. I gritted my teeth, knowing that soon the road widened into two lanes. I whipped around another crazy turn and the road suddenly widened, giving the SUV room to pass.

"Ha!" I yelled, easing up on the gas. "Go on by, jerk!"

The SUV stayed behind me for another five seconds as I slowed down, then pulled into the other lane and sped up. The driver pulled parallel to me, jerked the wheel, and the side of the SUV loomed in my face. I again prepared to die as I drove the 4-Runner dangerously close to the shoulder of the road. I had exhausted any more pavement, but the SUV suddenly pulled into the left lane and raced forward. Before it disappeared, I noticed that the left taillight was broken. Last Friday night, someone paid me a visit complete with a baseball bat beating. That someone was sending a message again.

I slowed to a stop and parked on the side of the road, at once furious and grateful. For a moment I clenched the wheel and shook violently. A dark thought occurred to me. Maybe the X Women were after me, too. I shuddered and forced myself to breathe evenly. After a minute, I pulled carefully back onto the road and drove home, more fearful than I'd been in a long time.

CHAPTER FOURTEEN

"What?" I mumbled into the telephone the next morning. I squinted at the big red numbers on the clock. Six a.m.

"Here's what I found out." Cal hasn't many social graces.

"Do you know what time it is?"

"Uh, it's early," Cal said. "Listen, I've been up all night, and I've found out a few things about that, uh, situation."

I sat up in bed. "Cal, you don't need to be so clandestine. It's not like my phones are tapped."

"Yeah, that's probably true." Cal paused and I heard papers rattling in the background. I could picture him trying to find the dozens of scraps of paper that he typically took notes on. "How much do you know about money laundering and that sort of thing?"

"Only what I see in the movies," I chuckled. "Are the X Women into money laundering as well as murder?"

"Sort of," Cal answered. "Here's the two-dollar version of what they do. With that much money being passed around, and not for legitimate business affairs, the group has to have a way of accessing it without anyone interfering. That's where the Cayman Islands come in."

"I'm with you so far."

"The money is deposited in a bank in the Caymans. Now you need a legitimate business in order to make this all work. So you buy a corporation in the Caymans or somewhere in Europe. There are probably others, too. Anyway, you can buy a corporation cheap; I found a number of ways of doing this. Once your corporation is set up, you borrow money against that corporation, set up a legitimate business, and make your deposits as profit from the business. Money launderers do this all the time. Maybe they buy a restaurant or something, and at the end of each month, they deposit money from their drug deals or whatever with the real profits. Now you can use the money from illegitimate sources, and no one's the wiser."

"But that can be tracked, can't it?"

"Sometimes, but once the feds figure out what the criminals are doing, the criminals change the way they do things."

"Always one step ahead."

"Exactly. And if you put enough layers around yourself, it makes it that much harder to get caught. Think of it like an onion. If the real source of the money is at the center of the onion, and you have numerous businesses and banks involved, each one a layer around the center, you have to peel a lot of onion skin before you get to the truth."

"So how are the X Women involved in money laundering?" I asked.

"Well, I suspect it's not like you think of money laundering, like the Mafia, but they do use the same type of system so no one knows about them." I heard more paper rattling. "I traced that account number Amanda gave you to a bank in the Cayman Islands. She deposited five hundred thousand dollars to an account back in December. The name on the account is 'Ultionis Femina'."

"That sounds like Latin or something."

"It is, Reed."

"They weren't even trying to fool anyone with that name," I said. "Can you imagine naming your daughter that?"

Cal chuckled. "No, especially when you learn the meaning. I looked it up. It roughly translates into 'avenging woman'. The address the woman provided was 3241 Five Book Way."

"Hang on, let me write that down." I sat up and grabbed a pad and pen I keep handy on the nightstand. Cal repeated the address, spelling the street name for me. "Funny name," Cal said. "I found a number of Book Avenues, and Book Ways, but not Five Book. I didn't find that street listing anywhere, not that that's a surprise." I studied it while he talked.

"I'll bet it means something," I yawned, still trying to wake up.

"Yep." Cal never talks in a know-it-all tone, but when he knows it all, you just know that he knows. "You already figured this out," I said.

"Yep."

"Okay, let me think here. I'm not at my peak before the sun rises." Cal didn't respond. I had a sudden flash. "Did you look that up in a Bible?"

Cal snorted. "Good idea."

"What's the fifth book in the Bible? Not Genesis. Numbers?"

"Keep guessing."

I scratched my chin. "Deuteronomy? Is that the fifth book in the Bible?"

"Very good, Holmes." I rolled over on my side, and felt around under the bed to find the Bible my mother had given me. I blew the dust off of it and coughed.

"It hasn't seen much use, huh?" Cal asked.

"No, to my mother's chagrin," I said. "Let's see." I cradled the phone with my shoulder and turned to Deuteronomy, chapter 32, verse 41. "*When I sharpen my flashing sword and my hand grasps it in judgment, I will take vengeance on my adversaries and repay those who hate me.*"

"These women are creative, if nothing else."

"And scary. They're not leaving much to the imagination."

"I wouldn't want to run into them in a dark alley," Cal said.

"Since you rarely leave your house, I don't think that's a problem."

"Yeah, right. Anyway, I searched for anything on 'Ultionis Femina', but didn't find anything on her, either here or in the Cayman Islands. Not that I expected to, but you never know. And you know how simple it is to create fake names, identities, the whole works. So I continued with the money trail instead. Amanda's funds were rewired that afternoon to an account in Lucerne, Switzerland. The money was withdrawn from that account a day later. The name on that account is Wilma O. Trace."

"Wilma O. Trace?" I pondered that for a second as I wrote it down. Then it made perfect sense. "Oh, I get it. Without a trace."

"They are cute, aren't they?" Cal chuckled again. "Same thing with that name. Nothing. And the money trail disappeared, too. It's all that layering going on. They essentially vanish."

"Without a trace." I pulled the covers up over me, getting more comfortable. "This is a well-connected group," I said. "It still takes a bit of rope-pulling and power in order to set all this up. It takes a good bit to put together fake I.D.'s, credit cards, Social Security numbers, and who knows what else for a bunch of people."

"I spent quite a while searching for the X Women," Cal continued. "Once I got past the porn sites, I contacted a number of sources," his polite way of saying computer hackers, "but it was a dead end."

"Too bad," I said.

"No, I really mean a dead end," Cal repeated. "I've never seen a bunch of geeks get so frightened all of a sudden. And these guys break the law all the time, so it's not like this should've scared them. But it did. I finally got one of the guys, Scatter D, to talk with me a little bit in one of the chat rooms, and he said he's heard a few things here and there, but he wasn't saying much. He did say that people who talk end up dead. Reed, this organization of yours does not mess around. They remind me of the Mafia."

"It's not my group," I said. "Please, I want nothing to do with them, especially if they're like the Mafia. Hey, I didn't tell you what happened to me last night on my way home." I proceeded to relate my adventure with the SUV.

"You should get out, now."

"I wish I could." I heard Cal let out a huge sigh.

"I'll be careful, Mom."

"Your mother would say the same thing," Cal said.

"I know."

"I'll keep looking. Go back to bed."

I tried, but I couldn't get what Cal had said off my mind.

CHAPTER FIFTEEN

There was no way I was falling back asleep. I was wide awake after my conversation with Cal, and this new information was running a race in my head. I pulled on a pair of sweats and plodded barefoot into the bathroom. I splashed cold water on my face, and carefully took the butterfly bandages off the cut on my temple. It seemed to be healing well, so I cleaned the wound but didn't bother to reapply bandages. I'd have a small scar, but nothing more. I smiled at myself in the mirror and sauntered into the kitchen where I fixed coffee. The aroma of the gourmet beans filled the kitchen, and I took a steaming cup into my home office.

I don't indulge in many things, but my office is one of them. It's a cozy room with floor-to-ceiling bookshelves on one wall where I keep most of my prized possessions. I have a DVD case full of my favorite detective movies, along with a collection of Alfred Hitchcock classics. The bookshelves are packed with a ton of books, mostly murder mysteries, and a collection of rare first edition detective novels.

I set the coffee down and started up my computer, and

began an Internet search on "Janet Delacroix". Maggie had given me little information about the football player she claimed to have helped eliminate, but I had her daughter's name. That would be my starting point.

I typed in 'female student murdered' and received a list of more than fourteen thousand matches. I needed to narrow the search, so I typed in the name Janet Delacroix. This brought the list to a measly five websites. I quickly scanned the high-lighted search words, and the associated web link, and deter-mined that, except for the last one, none fit my criteria. The last one took me to a website for the National Library of Medi-cine, with Janet listed as an employee in the research depart-ment. If it was the same Janet, Maggie's daughter, she lived in the Washington, D.C. area. That didn't help me in finding out about her murdered friend, but contacting her might be a possi-bility, if I wanted to follow that trail. I thought about my Internet search. I'd gone too broad, then too narrow, now could I find something in the middle?

I took out 'Janet Delacroix', kept the words 'female student murdered' and added 'college'. Still over seven thousand. I added 'football star'. This narrowed the search to a thousand. I checked a number of the websites, but none had anything to do with a girl murdered by a college football star. I mulled over how to narrow the search even further while I sipped my coffee. I scrolled through another page and was about to start a new search when one website caught my eye. It was an archived article from the Miami Herald about a university student murdered near the school campus, and how that had an influ-ence on campus safety at some Florida college campuses. The article wasn't specific to the murder, and didn't mention the school or the student. I added the words 'Florida' and changed 'college' to 'university'. Now I had a little over a hundred.

Not only was the list more manageable, I was hitting a

number of archived articles about the murder of a university student. Unfortunately the websites were for newspapers that wanted a fee to check the articles, or I could request a hard copy that would be sent in the mail. I didn't have time for that, so I kept scrolling down the screen, clicking on each website and scanning the web page. After the first ten or so, I began to doubt my research methods. By twenty, I began to devise ways to get Maggie to divulge the information. *Tell me or I'll force you to wear polyester*.

On twenty-eight, I hit gold.

"Murder of popular teenager has police puzzled," read the teaser line under the website address. I clicked on the link. The logo for *The Gainesville Sun* appeared on the top of the page, with "archives" in bold letters underneath. Six articles were listed on the page, and I didn't have to pay to check the articles. I held my breath as I clicked on the first link and opened the article.

Two sentences into the article I knew this was the one. The article was about a nineteen-year-old woman named Elaine Richards, found murdered on November 1, 2006. Her semi-nude body had been discovered near Lake Alice, close to the University of Florida. She had extensive bruising around her neck, and rape was suspected. The police were not releasing further details until after an autopsy could be performed.

The next article had even more information. The night before the discovery of her body, Elaine and her boyfriend, Derek Jones, star linebacker for the University of Florida Gators, spent the evening together. When I read the name, a vague memory popped into my mind. I'm not a big fan of college football, but I seemed to remember something about the incident because the announcers for one of the Bowl games mentioned how Derek's potential pro football career had been in jeopardy because of the murder and his possible culpability in it.

The couple had gone out to dinner on Halloween night at a posh restaurant near the university. The waiter and maitre'd both remembered Derek eating there with a pretty girl, but could offer little else about them. Elaine's roommate and best friend, who wanted to remain anonymous, hadn't expected her friend to come home at the end of the evening, and hadn't worried until Elaine didn't show up for a ten a.m. class they shared. Elaine's roommate still hadn't told anyone of Elaine's disappearance when the nightly news reported finding the body of a woman on the shore of Lake Alice, near the university's nature preserve. Elaine's roommate had a gut feeling and went to the police. She identified the body.

Poor kid, I thought of Janet Delacroix. Barely an adult and being thrust into a situation like that. The rest of the story centered on the lack of clues in the investigation, and how the police had initially suspected Derek Jones, but dismissed him after his roommate and another friend provided an alibi for him.

I read the other articles, each shorter than the last. Cause of death was asphyxiation caused by being choked, most likely with a belt. She had been raped, and due to bruises on her back, wrists, legs and face, beating and possible torture were also suspected. The police lamented the lack of clues and leads, and the campus population was on edge. The last, tiny article said that Elaine's funeral was being held out-of-state, and that the police still had no leads or suspects.

Now that I had a name, I searched on "Elaine Richards" and "Derek Jones", and came up with some more articles that didn't divulge much more than what I already knew. One victory was the mention of the detective in charge of the investigation, George Romero from the Gainesville Police Department.

I spent a few minutes finding the number for the police department in Gainesville, Florida. It was a few minutes after eight, Denver time. As I dialed the number for the Gainesville PD I hoped that George was both still employed with the department and available.

A woman with a slow drawl informed me that George Romero had retired. Maybe that was a good thing – a retired cop might be more likely to talk to me about an old case. After thanking her and hanging up, I searched phone directories in the area and found a couple of George Romeros. Now I just had to hope one of them was the former detective.

I struck out the first time. "Please be the right George," I whispered as I dialed the next number.

"George Romero." A deep voice rumbled into the phone.

"George, my name is Philip Marlowe," I said, using the name of the fictional detective in *The Big Sleep*. "I'm with the Boulder Police Department." After Jon Benet, I didn't need to identify the state. Everyone at all related to criminal investigation knew of Boulder, Colorado.

"Yes?"

"You were the detective investigating the death of Elaine Richards, correct?"

"Yes sir, that's true." I did a silent high five into the air.

"I'm sorry to bother you, but I'm wondering if I can ask you a few questions?"

"What can I do for you?" Polite, but cautious.

"I'm investigating a rape case that took place near the college here, and some of my research into similar cases around college campuses led me to one you investigated a few years ago, a woman by the name of Elaine Richards."

"Yes sir, I remember that case. The unsolved ones can stick with you." His voice boomed so that I held the receiver an inch from my ear. "She was a popular young lady, had quite a future in front of her. One of those cases you hate to see."

"Why did the case remain unsolved?" I asked.

"We didn't have anything to go on." He stretched out his words as he spoke. "I looked first at Derek Jones – you familiar with him?" I said I was and he continued. "Of course, you always look at the husband or boyfriend, right? But he had an airtight alibi, so I had to look elsewhere. And we didn't have that much to work with. We think the killer, or killers, dropped her body there after she'd been raped and killed."

"What about forensic evidence?"

"Very little of that. The perp, or perps, used condoms because the autopsy didn't find any sperm, even though she was violated. Hair and fiber results came up with very little as well. No DNA evidence. Whoever murdered that poor girl must have read a lot of detective fiction. They were careful. Really careful," he mused.

"So after Derek Jones, did you have any other suspects?"

"We checked into a few boys she dated that fall, but never did get enough on anybody to take it to the D.A. You know how that goes."

I concurred. "You mentioned that Derek had an airtight alibi."

"Yes sir, his roommate and his best friend both swear he was with them after he took Elaine home. All three said they dropped Elaine off at her dorm. They watched her disappear through the front door and they left. We checked around the dorm and found a few students who remember the car, a black Firebird, driving through the parking lot at the time those boys said they were there. No one specifically remembers Elaine getting out of the car, but it was dark, and the witnesses saw the car, not the people in it. I tried to find loopholes in Derek's alibi, but I couldn't."

"You think Derek did it," I said.

Romero breathed heavily into the phone. "That wasn't a popular viewpoint around here, him being a football player, and a good one at that." I waited for him to continue, hoping he would share what he really thought. He finally spoke. "Yes sir, I think that boy was guilty. He raped and murdered that girl. I'd hang my badge on it."

"Why so sure?"

"My gut told me those other boys were lying for him, giving Derek his alibi so he wouldn't take the rap. And when I looked into his background, he wasn't the all-American boy that he appeared to be. He had a history of violence, some bar brawls, and some allegations from a former girlfriend."

"None of that was ever reported?" I asked, thinking about the articles I'd just read. This did not fit the football star described by the papers.

"No sir. Derek had that little girl scared silly. She never pressed charges, never said anything to her parents, or any authorities. I stumbled on it when I interviewed some of the girls in Elaine's dorm; would've missed it otherwise. That girl told me she'd deny it if I reported it or said anything public about it. Now she may've been lying, but my gut says no way."

I pondered that for a moment. "So the case remains unsolved?"

"That's right. And it'll probably remain that way."

"Why?"

Romero grunted. "You know what happened to Derek Jones?"

"No," I said.

"Derek was driving down Highway 75 two nights after he played in the national championship game. He had two interceptions in that game, played just great. Maybe he was still celebrating. Anyway, he ran his truck straight into a guardrail, and down an embankment. He was thrown from the car, killed instantly."

"It was an accident?" I couldn't contain my surprise. I naturally assumed the X Women wouldn't worry about covering up a murder.

"Yes sir, an accident. And I can't say that I mourn his passing," Romero said.

Silence filled the phone line between us. "What's this case that you're working on?" Romero finally asked.

"Oh, I can't divulge any information right now," I said. He murmured understanding. "But I appreciate your help."

"My pleasure," he said. "I hope that helps you in your investigation."

"Let's hope so," I said truthfully.

"What was your name?"

"Philip Marlowe," I said.

"Isn't that the name of a detective from an old book or something?"

"Yes," I said. "My mother was a fan of the old classics. Hey, thanks again," I said and hung up the phone.

CHAPTER SIXTEEN

I must've sat at my desk for ten minutes mulling over my conversation with George Romero. So the X Women made Derek's death look like an accident. This group looked more and more like one that operated with a cold efficiency, swooping down like Spiderman, I thought wryly, to mete out justice, then leaving without a trace of ever having been there. I wondered how many other murders the X Women committed in the name of justice, murders that they made look like an accident.

I plodded to the kitchen for a fresh cup of coffee, then returned to the computer. I ran some searches, trying to come up with a way of finding accidental deaths of people who had recently been accused of a crime, or had been convicted of a crime. I didn't have much luck, hitting way too many websites that had nothing remotely to do with my search. I also had a difficult time getting a reasonable list. Most searches resulted in thousands of hits. I sat back, thinking of how I could glean this information from the World Wide Web. There was only one thing to do.

"Hey, aren't you going to get some sleep?" I asked when Cal picked up the phone.

"Tonight. I've got some work to get done." He didn't even sound tired.

"Have you come up with anything more on the X Women?"

"I just got off the phone with you a couple of hours ago," he said. "I have a client who's screaming to get his software back tomorrow. I need to work on that for awhile, then I'll look into it some more." Cal's work as a consultant allowed him to work from home, but I didn't understand much of what he did. He once told me his work was similar to Sandra Bullock's in *The Net* and I took his word for it.

"You're not going to believe what I found out since you called," I said.

"That you drool in your sleep?" Cal asked. The sound of him tapping on his keyboard clacked through the phone while we talked. "Want me to find out more about the X Women? Are they really women? Or does the X stand for women who've had sex change operations, hence they are ex-women? See it on the next Jerry Springer."

"Ha, ha," I said. "I tracked down another victim of the X Women."

"You're counting Peter Ghering as a victim?"

"Yeah, besides him." The clicking stopped, which meant I had his full attention. "I've been on the Internet, and I finally tracked down Maggie's friend, the girl she says was killed by a football star."

"I really thought you'd go back to bed."

"I couldn't sleep after everything you told me." I relayed to him my last couple of hours of work, ending with George Romero's tale. "I need to find out if there's been other accidental deaths of people who've been accused or convicted of a violent crime, or who have served time for something like that, then got out and died in mysterious circumstances."

"That's your working theory?"

"So far. I know it's thin, but..."

"Uh huh," Cal said, before lapsing into silence. I could almost hear the wheels grinding in his head as he thought. "It wouldn't just be violent crimes. I'd bet the X Women have committed murder for other things as well."

"That's what I would assume," I said. "But I can't find anything on just the violent crimes. If I broaden my search that much, I'll never find anything. It's just a starting place, to see if I can find a pattern."

"I'll take care of that for you," Cal said. "I'll just add it to the X Women list."

"What are you going to do?" I asked, then immediately said, "No, I don't want to know."

"It's nothing bad," Cal chuckled. "I have more resources at my fingertips, and I know where to look. You just play on the computer." Compared to Cal's computer skills, I had to agree. "Come up here later and we'll see what we can find."

"Sure, how about later this afternoon?" He grunted a response, which I took to be a 'yes' and I hung up. That done, I padded into the kitchen with my empty coffee cup, then showered and dressed.

———

After I got cleaned up, I ate a bagel, and walked over to the office. I didn't have much to do there, just check my messages and retrieve the mail. I wondered, not for the first time, about spending so much for rent on an office I rarely saw, but I held hopes of a burgeoning business. Besides, I needed an office to show my father that I was legitimate. The voicemail system had a call from a prospective client, a man who wanted to set up an appointment with me after he returned from Barbados. He'd call again in two weeks. Another prospect. All right then.

I turned on the stereo, booted up my computer, and made some notes about the case so far. In the midst of finding out about the X Women, I had shoved Peter Ghering to the back of my mind. Where was he? And the bigger question, was he still alive?

I called Detective Jimmy Merrick. The dispatcher put me through to him. When I identified myself, his tone turned cautiously curious. "You're still helping that Ghering woman?" He couldn't have sounded more derisive of her.

"Let's just say that I have my own interest in the case," I said.

"Okay," he agreed. "We'll say that. What do you want from me?"

He certainly came right to the point. No BS, just like the night I'd met him at Amanda's. "I know you don't think much of Amanda." His silence spoke volumes about his opinion of her. "But what do you think happened to Peter Ghering? Do you have anything more?"

A chair squeaked in the background, and I could picture Merrick shifting his powerful frame. "I can't tell you anything." He spoke as if he didn't believe his own weak bluff.

"Sure you can, if you want," I said. "I promise not to bug you if you tell me what you've got."

"Hey, buddy, I'm the one who'll be crawling up your behind if you step over the line." He let out a sigh that sounded more like a wheeze, as he played the Reluctant Game. "All right, I guess it can't harm anything to tell you that we haven't turned anything up yet. We've been in contact with the feds in Philly, and they haven't gotten any unidentified male bodies, or anything else that would lead us to believe Peter was murdered and left there. He hasn't turned up here, at least as far as I know. Amanda might be able to tell you more."

"What do you mean?"

"It wouldn't surprise me if she's holding out on all of us." I'm sure my silence now told him that I agreed. "On the record, I don't have anything to go on, so there's not much I can do."

"Off the record?" I asked.

"My own opinion, he got the hell away from that crazy woman. Officially, he's a missing person."

"Any leads?"

"None. He hasn't used a credit card since that Monday."

"Monday?"

"Is there an echo? That's what I said. Monday. He pulled out a cash withdrawal of five hundred from an ATM in downtown Philly. Near the Liberty Bell. We don't have anything else."

"Which credit card?" I thought about Amanda's calls to her credit card companies. She hadn't said anything about that transaction. I wondered how many lies of hers I would uncover before I found Peter.

"Am-Ex. It was his business account. You want anything else, Sherlock?"

I ignored the gibe, thanked Merrick and hung up. If Peter was slated to be killed on Monday, before he left Philadelphia, did this confirm he'd gotten away? Unless someone else used his card instead. I shuddered at the thought. Today was Wednesday. More than a week had passed since Peter disappeared. Was he alive or dead?

I took care of some busy work, mostly stuff I concocted, ate a late lunch at Jason's Deli, and drove up to Cal's house about three o'clock. As I made each winding curve, I couldn't help but envision last night's journey, hurtling down the mountain. What had been gaping blackness now showed up as the jagged sides of valleys sloping down from the highway. Had I gone over the edge, it would not have been a pretty death. But it would have been made to look like an accident, I thought. The signature kill for the X Women.

"Don't you ever work?" Cal said when he opened the door. Before I could answer he was shuffling back down the hallway to his office. Judging by his matted hair, wrinkled shirt, and cheap cologne, Cal hadn't bothered to shower or change clothes. Personal hygiene took a back seat when Cal pursued a new project.

I followed him into his sanctuary and plopped onto the love seat. "I am working." The usual dust cloud swirled into the air when my butt hit the cushions. I settled back. "I'm working with you."

He wagged his head as he swiveled around to face one of the monitors. "I've got something on that thing." He was being clandestine again.

"The X Women?" I asked.

"Yeah." He started punching away at the keyboard, hunched over.

I sat up. "Anything good?"

"I've come up with some possible accidents that they could've been involved in. I've created a list." He printed a document and handed it to me.

"How did you do this?" I got up and started to pace, reading the paper. It had a list of names, all male, a date next to the name, and the cause of death. I held up a hand. "Wait, no, I don't want to know how you did it." I sat back down.

"Quit worrying," he said. "It is possible to get information without hacking." I began rubbing my eyes nervously. "Do you want to know what I found out?" He held up numerous pieces of scrap paper, his way of organization.

"Why didn't you put it in the document?"

He held up his hands in exasperation, pitching the paper

pieces back onto the desk. "I didn't get that far. Do you want to know what I've got here?"

"What?"

He rolled his chair closer to me. "Going back ten years, I found at least seven accidents." He used his fingers, making quotation marks when he said the word "accidents". "Each one could've been just that, an accident. But all of them could've been murder. Things like car crashes, a suicide, a hunting accident, and the most interesting one was a guy who apparently was into kinky sex. He liked that auto-erotic asphyxiation thing."

"You strangle yourself while you're masturbating," I said in plain English.

"Right. It's very dangerous, or even deadly. That was the case for this guy."

"Okay, that kind of sex is unusual, but why is this guy special?"

He leaned toward me, intent on his revelations. "I know it happens, a lot more lately. But here's what makes this particular case stick out." If he intended on making a pun, he didn't show it. "It happened in New York City, at a Manhattan brokerage house. The guy, name of Rick Gerardo, had been acquitted in a rape case two months previous to his death. He was accused of raping a woman that he worked with. According to the story, they'd been getting it on in his office after hours, but after a few months, she broke it off. He wasn't happy with that, and she accused him of forcing himself on her one Friday evening after work."

I pursed my lips, thinking it over. "That could tie in, but it's shaky." I rubbed my eyes again. "Ah, hell. This whole thing is shaky."

He leaned even closer, adamant. "No, listen. This is the tie-in. Guess what kind of sex they liked to have?"

I tipped my head up slowly. "Ah. Kinky sex."

"Not just kinky. Auto-erotic asphyxiation. They both testified to that in court."

"But what about the rape? Was it really forced or was she holding a grudge against him? Trying to get back at him for something, so she accuses him of rape. That's what I would wonder."

He shrugged. "From the articles I read, it sounds like that's the line the jury took. They didn't believe the prosecution proved force, so they acquitted. But according to court testimony, the woman said Rick was brutal that night. According to her, he nearly killed her while he raped her, that he choked her with the intent to kill, not just for the sexual rush. And he was her boss, so after she broke it off, he threatened her with her job."

"Apparently that didn't work," I observed.

"Right. She went ahead and accused him publicly, lost her job, was humiliated by having to tell the story in court, then was blackballed by the company and its associates. Her statement after the trial said she was leaving New York, going back to Delaware to live with her parents for a while."

"And devise a means of punishing Rick, if this is an X Women case."

"Right." Cal sat back with a satisfied look on his face. "I researched the family some. Daddy is a prominent attorney in Delaware, and they're old money."

"So they could afford to hire the X Women," I finished.

Cal clapped his hands once in triumph. "And the other cases I found are similar. If possible, the death was made to mirror the crime of the accused. I haven't got all the details, but I can work on that tonight."

I didn't say anything for a minute. "This organization is slick," was all I could come up with.

"You said it," Cal concurred. "Now it could all be coincidence, but you never know. And I've only been at this a little while. Who knows what I might find with some more time."

"You want to grab a bite to eat?" I switched topics.

"No, I've got too much going on here to stop."

I smiled at his dedication. "Keep at it, then." I stood up to leave.

He smiled. "Sure. This is more fun than looking for viruses in software."

"And don't forget to eat something fresh." I held up a bowl with a substance that once might have been cereal, but now was a congealed blob. He stared at me blankly and turned back to the computer.

CHAPTER SEVENTEEN

Late afternoon shadows were already turning to darkness as I left Cal's house, and I smelled a crisp coldness in the air. I had an uneventful drive down the mountain, even though I kept checking my rearview mirror for suspicious SUVs. In forty minutes I was pulling the 4-Runner in the alley garage I shared with the Goofball brothers. Deuce's battered Ford truck sat in the other space, so he was home from work.

I got out and closed the garage door, then trudged through the back yard and around the building to the front porch. I was headed for the side entrance to my condo when Ace came out.

"You wanna go with us to B-52's?" he asked. "We were thinking about shooting some pool."

"That sounds like fun," I answered. It had been a long day, and I didn't need much convincing.

Deuce leaped out onto the porch, his heavy gray overcoat and black gloves already on. "How's business?" he asked with a goofy grin on his face.

"Trying to help a lady find her missing husband," I explained in simple terms.

"Hmm," Deuce mused. "Is that stuff exciting?"

"Not usually," I said as we started walking down the street.

"Like in the movies?" This from Ace.

"Yeah," I smiled. Humphrey Bogart, eat your heart out.

"Those movies you like, are they any good?" Deuce asked.

"They're great. All the action, the subplots, and the actors. Bogie, Edward G. Robinson, Burt Lancaster. Beautiful women and mysterious twists and turns."

"Bogie?" Ace said. "Why are we talking golf?"

"We aren't," I said.

"Weren't we talking about some movie?" Deuce asked.

I looked up into blank faces. "Forget it."

Ace put an arm around my shoulder. "Nah, man. You like those movies, maybe we should watch one."

"Yeah, whaddaya recommend?" Deuce asked.

I smiled, thinking about Bogie, the coolest of the cool detectives. "*The Big Sleep.* That's film noir at its best."

"Film what?" Ace said.

"Film noir. It's a genre...Forget it." The blank stares told me I'd lost them again. "I like that one, although I don't know if you guys would. It's kind of complicated."

"Hey, if you like it, we should watch it," Deuce said.

"*The Big Sleep*," Ace said. "We got that down at the store. I can get it."

"I've got the DVD if you want to borrow it." I really doubted they would get it, all the subtleties and dark subplots, but it might broaden their horizons. At least it had lots of action, and lots of people getting killed. And Lauren Bacall, she was one hot babe.

Ace smiled. "I can get it for free, so it's no problem."

"Connections," Deuce said wisely.

"You have some phone work or cable done on your place?" Deuce asked abruptly, picking the question out of the air.

"Hmm?" I mumbled.

"Are you changing your cable or something?" Deuce changed his phrasing, as if that would help me understand him.

"No. Why?"

"I saw a guy going up to your place a few days ago. Drove up in a Comcast truck, had a tool kit with him. You know, he looked like a cable guy or something." Comcast provided my cable, but I didn't have any service work scheduled. My cable worked fine, but the alarms in my head were ringing loudly.

"When was this?" I stopped and grabbed Deuce's arm.

Deuce grimaced, thinking hard. "Last Friday. Early afternoon. I saw him when I came home for lunch."

My eyes flitted around, and I felt my senses shift into overdrive. Was someone watching me? Was I being followed? Did someone actually break into my house?

"Did he go around back?" I asked.

"No. He went up the steps to your place. He was in there for at least half an hour." A puzzled look crossed Deuce's face. "You didn't change your cable?"

"What'd he look like?"

Deuce shrugged his shoulders. "I dunno. Kind of tall, I guess. Like the cable guys, you know."

"I've got to go," I said, turning back.

"Hey, man. I didn't mean to make you mad," Deuce had a hurt look on his face.

I calmed down. "No, you didn't. There's something I have to check."

"Okay," he said cautiously. "We'll be at B 52's if you want to join us."

"Thanks," I called over my shoulder.

"We'll get that movie," Ace yelled back at me. "I hope it's as good as you say."

"So do I," I hollered back, leaving them to their fun.

I ran back home, Deuce's words drumming in my brain the whole way. I took the side stairs two at a time up to my door and just as I was about to put the key in the lock, I thought about electronic devices. The only reason I could think of for someone to be in my home was to plant a bug. Spy equipment. To listen to me. A pounding began in the back of my eyes, brought on by adrenaline, and maybe some fear. I was stepping into the big leagues.

I looked at the key in my hand. The second I opened the door, someone would know I had come home. Maybe they were watching me right now. I flipped around and stared down the steps, onto the street below. The moon, milky white and round as a marble, cast the street in a hazy glow. Then a car came down the street, moving slowly. It stopped and backed up, parallel parking across the street. The engine died and Willie Rhoden, my neighbor across the street, got out.

"Hey Reed, why are you staring at me? I told you I have a boyfriend." Willie, real name Willimena, was a nurse at St. Joseph's Hospital, just east of our neighborhood. She was twenty-eight, built like a marathon runner, and very attached to her boyfriend, Alan.

"Sorry, I thought you were someone else." I couldn't believe I didn't recognize her car. My suspicion meter was crossing into the red zone.

"Right." She started up her front walk. "You were staring," she hollered. Any other time that would've been true. Okay, I have a crush on her, even if she has a boyfriend.

I watched her disappear into her house before I turned and, with a determination born out of false bravado, unlocked the door and entered my condo. I tiptoed into the living room and turned on a lamp on the end table. The whole time my eyes were scanning the walls, the furniture, the windows, the television, and the phone. Why had someone disguised as a cable guy been in my condo? Was there a bug somewhere in this room? Or camera equipment? A creepy feeling started from the base of my skull and zipped down my spine. I felt naked. And paranoid.

"Oh hell," I said, taking off my coat. I took a deep breath, let it out, and determined that the X Women were not going to scare me. Not this guy. I was like Bogie.

I began a search of the condo, starting in the living room, coaching myself with tough-guy talk. "They don't know who they're messing with," I mumbled. I began a search with the obvious, checking the television, the cables behind the entertainment center, and the cable box. I checked the phones, starting with the one in the living room, then the bedroom phone. I took apart each receiver and didn't see anything beyond the complex equipment. Nothing looked out of place.

I examined the bedroom thoroughly but didn't find a thing, no hidden cameras or recorders. Nothing.

I gave the living room, my office, and the kitchen the same treatment, looking everywhere for any signs of bugs or listening devices. I even looked inside the Tupperware in the cupboards. I came up empty-handed.

I finally stopped for a breather, falling Indian-style on the floor, rivulets of sweat crawling down my face. My living room resembled a scene from *The Conversation*, where Gene Hackman's character tears up his entire apartment looking for an elusive bug. I scanned the mess and then I gave up, thoroughly frustrated. I laid back, stretched out my legs, and stared at the ceiling. I must be getting extremely fearful. I'd let Deuce's comment about a cable guy send me on a wild goose chase. I should've known not to listen to a guy I dubbed as a goofball.

And then I saw it.

CHAPTER EIGHTEEN

In the center of the ceiling hangs a ceiling fan. The housing was in two parts, the lower housing screwed to the upper housing, which was then secured into the ceiling. The faux-brass motor is decorated with evenly spaced holes. In every fifth hole a screw secured the housing together. Except for one hole, where the spacing was only three holes apart. I got up and looked up at the fan. That one screw didn't resemble the others. It looked like a tiny glass eye.

I dragged a chair from the kitchen and stood on it, directly under the fan. Now I could peer up into the metal housing, right at the suspicious-looking screw. I was being watched by a tiny camera. I wondered which X Woman was staring back at me. And if they had planted a spying device, I was sure they would be listening as well. Judging by the mess in the condo, I was pretty sure a bug wasn't inside, but maybe outside, on the building or in the phone cables.

In my haste to go outside and look I nearly fell off the chair. Anger was taking over my sense of reason. The X Women were watching me, listening to me. I jerked open the door, ran out onto the little porch, and looked for the phone lines. I spotted them, coming from wires in the alley, attached to the overhang of the building then running down the side of the house. I dashed down the stairs, did a one-eighty around the rail, and started to run under the stairs toward the back yard. I ducked under an overhanging branch from one of the large oak trees on the side of the house and ran smack into the biggest man I had ever seen.

"Oof!" I swear that's exactly what I said. And after the "oof," I stumbled backward right into another man. I felt hands come under my shoulders and push me erect, and much closer to the Herculean guy than I cared to be.

"Mr. Ferguson, would you come with us, please?" The man behind me spoke in a resonating baritone. I slowly turned around, expecting another giant. Instead I was confronted by an average-looking, average-aged man. He could've been a businessman or a neighbor coming home from a long day at the office. Except for the gun in his right hand. I glanced at Hercules behind me. Moonlight beamed off of his completely bald head. His squared shoulders stretched the seams of a black wool overcoat and I saw a bulge in his left coat pocket. I debated my options, like running, or asking them upstairs for a beer.

As if he read my mind, Baritone said, "Let's not make this difficult, Mr. Ferguson." He spoke in a cultured manner. I'd bet money he was Ivy-League educated.

"I didn't know the X Women hired men," I countered, stalling for time. "I thought they just killed them." All the great detectives stall when they don't have a clue what to do next. And I was clueless.

"Come with us, please." Baritone gestured toward the street with the gun. A full-size, four-door SUV sat doubled-parked in front of the building. He strode off toward it, looking over his shoulder to ensure that I followed. I hesitated but then felt the breath of Hercules behind me, so I reluctantly made my way over to the vehicle. Hercules matched my every step, his shoes crunching loudly on the sidewalk. In the meantime, Baritone reached the SUV, opened the back door, and waited for me. As I neared him, he reached out and began searching me.

"You won't be needing this," he said, taking my cell phone. When he'd finished, he jerked his head toward the car.

I eyed him levelly as I climbed in the backseat. He had an amused look as he eyed me back.

Two men sat in the SUV, a driver and another solid-looking man on the other side of the back seat who wore a dark overcoat over a gray suit. He tipped his head once, then resumed staring at the back of the driver's head. Hercules got in right after me, scrunching me in the middle. Baritone got in the front seat and we took off down the street.

"So is somebody going to tell me what this is all about?" I asked.

No answers. We rode in silence until we got to 17th Avenue, where the driver turned right and headed east. After two lights, Baritone hiked himself around where he could see me.

"You've become a real liability." He smiled at me.

"That's what I was hired to do."

The smile turned into a slit. "No, Mr. Ferguson. You were hired to find Peter Ghering."

"I go where the trail leads me," I said, shifting to my left, trying to get some of Hercules weight off me. "It led straight to you guys. Or gals."

Baritone shook his head. "I may have given you more credit than you deserve, Mr. Ferguson. We don't work for the X Women. We're trying to find them. Just like you." I tensed slightly. "I'm Special Agent Dobson of the FBI."

"Yeah, right," I said. My nerves felt taut and adrenalin was pumping through my veins. I looked from Dobson to the guy on the left, who nodded once again but didn't introduce himself. I turned from him to Hercules. "Special Agent Jones," he said, speaking for the first time in a voice too high for his massive physique. He tried to stare me down, his dark eyes squinting at me.

I felt all my organs churning inside me, and hoped the agents couldn't hear them. I had my doubts that real agents would nab someone like they'd just done to me, but how could I question a gun pointed at me? I locked my jaw and narrowed my eyes in what I hoped was an intimidating posture. "If you're FBI agents, where are your badges?" With a trace of a smile on his face, Dobson pulled a black wallet from his coat pocket and flipped it open. I saw a golden shield with three initials carved into it, and an identification card underneath the shield. Jones did the same, and I scrutinized his ID as well. The guy on my left continued to gaze straight ahead, and I chose to let him continue doing that. I didn't need to see his badge to know that I was in a precarious situation. "They could be fakes," I said.

Dobson continued to look at me as he put his wallet away. "I had hoped that it wouldn't come to this..." He left the rest of the sentence for me to figure out.

"You've been watching me." I received a nod in answer. "Listening in?" Another nod. "Following me?" After all, I was riding in a black SUV, the same kind that I assumed had been following Amanda. Dobson nodded his head one final time. "Why'd you slug me over the head?" He stared at me. "And what about the following me home from Cal's, trying to run me off the road?"

"I assure you that was not us, but it is clear you are a danger to many people. As for our interest in you, once Amanda Ghering hired you, we had to know how successful you were," he said. "You really have been too smart for your own good.

Certainly too smart for ours. You're threatening our investigation. I won't allow that."

By now we had turned north onto Colorado Boulevard, past the Natural History Museum, IMAX Theater, and Denver Planetarium. "You got me into the car by using a gun? Isn't that illegal?" I asked. "What happened to my rights?"

Dobson chuckled. "That's a myth of all those detective shows you watch. If needed, I can stretch the rules."

"This is stretching?" I shifted again, elbowing Jones not so subtly in the side. He leaned into the door.

Dobson glanced out the windshield. I noted that we were now merging onto Interstate 70, going east again. "Where are you taking me?"

"All in due time." Dobson paused. "What happened to Peter Ghering?"

"I don't know. He's disappeared without a trace." I was puzzled by the question, though. If the FBI had been spying on me, why didn't they know about my progress in the investigation? "Let me see that badge again," I demanded.

Dobson ignored that. "We need to come to an understanding, Mr. Ferguson."

"Like what?"

"Like you need to let this investigation go. You need to let us do our job."

"No can do," I said. "I've had my life threatened, and I've come too far. I'm not stopping now."

"What have you learned about the X Women?" Dobson raised his voice. He shifted so I could see the gun in his shoulder holster.

"They have quite an organization and they are very adept at what they do. But you already know that."

"How did you find out about them?"

I chose my words carefully. "I noticed some unusual occurrences."

"What?"

"A pattern of accidental deaths happening to men who had been recently accused of a crime against a woman," I said.

"Who? What women?"

I crossed my arms defiantly. "That's all I'll say without a lawyer."

"I see." Dobson examined his fingernails thoughtfully. "As I've said, I have worked on this case for quite some time. Now I'm close to bringing this group down." He paused, then met my gaze. "And I won't allow you to jeopardize this." I stared back, waiting. "Do I make myself clear?"

"I'm not going to back off. Look, I've been lied to by the woman who hired me, knocked over the head, nearly run off a road, and now spied on by the FBI. If you think you can just tell me to 'let it go', as you say, you're crazy."

Dobson took a deep breath. "I can understand your reluctance to give up. But I must ask you again to not jeopardize our work. Do I make myself clear?" he repeated.

"I'm not a child."

His face stiffened. "Quite right. But I can ground you like one."

"You're going to sic Hercules on me?" I wagged my thumb at Jones.

"No." Dobson made a clicking sound. "I'm going to make it exceedingly uncomfortable for you if you continue."

"How?" By now we had passed Peña Boulevard, which leads to Denver International Airport. The area was becoming more barren the farther east we traveled. Only a few more exits and we would leave Denver behind and head toward Kansas. My mouth was suddenly dry, and I felt real fear grinding in my stomach. "Where are we going?"

"Sit tight, Mr. Ferguson. It will become clear." Dobson turned around and settled into his seat. I watched the back of his head for a moment, then peered to my left and right. The guy on the left seemed in a hypnotic state, focused on the seat back, while Jones appeared as bland as his name.

CHAPTER NINETEEN

We drove on in a chilling silence past the last exit to the eastern suburbs, into the darkness. I listened to my heart pounding and watched the mile markers pass by. Then the driver slowed, exited onto a frontage road, and followed this for a minute or two before turning down a dark dirt lane. The headlights illuminated a long stretch of road straight ahead, with no lights from houses or any other building visible. We traveled on the deserted road and after a mile or so, the vehicle stopped.

"Won't you join me outside?" Dobson said as he opened his door. Jones got out and held the door for me. "This way, Mr. Ferguson." Dobson walked down a slight incline at the edge of the road and waved me over. I had a sneaky suspicion that these guys weren't who they said they were, but I didn't have much choice except to go along.

I was flushed with fear even though it was frigidly cold. I stood rooted to my spot until Jones pushed me from behind. "Come on," he said. I stepped carefully, not sure of my footing as I followed Dobson. I tried to glance at the license plate on the SUV, but I couldn't make out the numbers on the dark plate. Besides, with Hercules prodding me on, I didn't have much time. I got to the bottom of the incline where Dobson stood waiting. He put his arm around my shoulders in a friendly gesture.

"Let's be reasonable about this," he said, like we were best friends chatting.

I didn't say a word. We started walking into a field, the uneven ground frozen under our feet.

"It's time for the games to end, Mr. Ferguson." We kept walking, the icy dirt crunching loudly under our feet. "Let the government handle this."

"And if I don't?"

Dobson stopped and faced me. His features were ghostly in the moonlight. He did not appear happy. "Things will get messy for you."

"Like what?"

"It doesn't take much to ruin a person, personally, financially, morally. I can make any of that happen. How would you like it if that trust fund of yours was suddenly eliminated?"

"I can handle it. I wouldn't be happy, but I'd work it out." I hoped he didn't hear the shaking in my voice. I crossed my arms against the cold, burying my hands in my armpits. "Money isn't everything."

Dobson moved in for the kill. "Maybe so, but what if I take down your family? Your friends? I can make things very complicated for Cal." His eyes narrowed. "He runs quite a little operation from his house in the foothills, doesn't he? I wonder just how much of it is legal. Maybe we should check into that."

A different kind of coldness swept over me. I couldn't let anything happen to my parents, nor could I let Cal get into trouble at my expense. "You're right to protect him." Dobson's smile chilled me more than the frigid air. "And you can. Just by leaving this investigation alone."

"You wouldn't," I said.

"Don't try me, Mr. Ferguson." He rocked back on his heels, signaling the end of our discussion. "Do I have your assurance that you leave this alone?"

I couldn't think of any alternatives. "Yes," I finally said.

"Stay away from Amanda Ghering. Do not see her. Do not communicate with her in any way."

"What if she calls me? I can't stop her from doing that."

"Let her know that you are no longer available to her. Understand?"

I nodded.

"Good." He seemed pleased with himself, clapping his hands together. "It is cold out here, isn't it? Too bad you rushed out without a coat." He turned and started back for the car. I took a few steps after him. Dobson turned around and held up his hand.

I stopped. "What now?"

"Our meeting is over, Mr. Ferguson."

"Okay, take me home." I pointed to the SUV. Dobson shoved his hands in his coat pockets, and even in the dark I could see him clutching the gun that was in the left pocket. He contemplated me in a nonchalant manner. My knees buckled under me and I almost fell down.

"What are you going to do?" I finally asked.

Dobson shrugged. "Stay away from this investigation. Stay away from Amanda Ghering. Stay away from anything that has to do with this organization. Do I make myself clear?"

"I said I would," I managed to say.

"Excellent choice." He turned his back to me again. "I will leave you to your own resources now," he called over his shoulder.

"You're going to leave me here?" I yelled after him. "If you're really the FBI, you wouldn't do that!"

He reached the SUV and in the moonlight I could see him say something to Jones, and then they both laughed.

"Hey!" I raised my voice even louder. Sensation came back into my legs and I began trotting toward the car. "You just threaten me and that's it?" I shouted, jabbing my finger into the air. "I have rights. I pay taxes." The men opened their car doors. "It's freezing out here!"

"I can do whatever I want," Dobson called out to me. "Let this be my warning to you."

"This doesn't happen in the movies!"

Dobson held a hand up. "This isn't a movie, Mr. Ferguson. Good night." The two men got into the car, slammed their doors, and the SUV pulled a quick U-turn, dipping down into a slope on the side of the road. The wheels spun for a second before catching traction, and the SUV roared off, spraying dirt behind it. I ran after it, swearing as many four-letter words as I could think of in the cold, but by the time I got to the road all I saw were two tiny red lights disappearing in the distance. And the left one was broken.

CHAPTER TWENTY

"Thanks for the ride," I said to the semi driver as he dropped me off at the side of the road near Interstate 70 and Quebec, on the eastern side of metro Denver. The big eighteen wheeler groaned as it edged its way back on the highway, leaving me in its dust.

Once I had determined that the SUV was not coming back for me, I ran back down the dirt road to the highway, yanking my flimsy sweater up around my ears, and stuffing my hands deep into the pockets of my jeans. That did little to keep out the burning cold, and I had to stop and walk twice because of stabbing pains in my side. I definitely needed to get in shape if I were going to continue in this profession.

I reached the highway, cold and out of breath. I crossed the eastbound lanes, ran through a grassy, frost-covered median, and began walking along the westbound lanes. I stuck my left arm out and pointed my thumb up, hoping someone would have pity on me. Cars hurtled by, but none stopped or even slowed down. After ten minutes my arm was tired, and I was fuming. The broken taillight told me one thing: the X Women were posing as the FBI. That thought made me grow colder still. I was lucky to be alive.

I was composing sentence after sentence of creative curses for the X Women, the FBI, and the imposter agent Dobson in particular, when a big rig slowed down ahead of me. The young driver seemed disappointed that I wanted a ride only to the nearest telephone. He'd have to look for someone else for company.

He dropped me within walking distance of a 7-Eleven that we spotted from the highway. I jogged to the pay phone on the side of the building and dug change from my pocket. My hands shook as I fed quarters into the pay slot. I punched in a number and waited. Three rings.

"Hello?"

"Deuce, it's me," I said through chattering teeth.

"Hey, Reed. We're done playing pool."

No kidding. "I need you to do me a favor."

"Sure. What do you need?"

"Can you come pick me up?"

"Uh, sure Reed. But why do you want me to pick you up?"

"I'm across town." I gave him directions to where I was.

"Oh. Okay," he said. "I'll leave right now."

I hung up and entered the store. I used the restroom and bought hot chocolate, never so grateful for a warm cup in my hands. I chatted with the clerk, who seemed wary of me. He didn't need to worry. If I robbed him of anything, it would be his coat.

I wished Deuce would hurry. Twenty minutes later, a white, full-size Chevy truck pulled up outside, and Deuce waved at me from the passenger window. It took a second before I realized that his brother, Bob, was driving the truck. I thanked the clerk as I left, and he seemed relieved that I wasn't going to do anything to him.

Deuce opened the truck door and scooted over into the middle seat. "Thanks for helping me out," I said as I got into the truck. I felt like I'd crawled into a fireplace. I put my hands gratefully in front of the heating vents as Bob hit the gas pedal.

"Somebody playing a joke on you?" Bob asked as we chugged out of the lot.

"Something like that," I said.

"Why are you all the way out here without your car?" Deuce glanced at me. "And your coat. You got mad at me the other day for not having my coat, remember?"

"Uh-huh," I said. "I'll make sure to follow my own advice next time."

"Is this about your job?" Deuce asked, a touch of worry in his voice.

The last thing I wanted to do was complicate his life with my work. Not that he would understand it. *I* didn't understand it. "Yeah, Deuce. It's no big deal, though," I answered.

Deuce seemed to buy that, crossing his arms and launching into small talk about his pool game. Bob listened with a wry smile on his face. I sank into the seat and was nearly asleep by the time we got home.

"You gonna watch the rest of the movie?" Deuce asked Bob as we walked up the porch steps.

"No, buddy, I've got to be up early tomorrow," Bob answered him.

"Okay. Don't forget dinner this weekend." Deuce said, punching Bob on the arm. "And you be careful," Deuce said to me in an eerie imitation of me warning him. Spooky.

"I will," I said as he disappeared inside. I turned to Bob. "Thanks again."

"I know I don't know you well, but should I be worried about you?" Bob asked. "First someone gives you a nasty bump on the head, then someone takes you on a ride into the middle of nowhere."

I hesitated a second, surprised by his concern. "No, I'm fine. All part of the job."

His eyes twinkled. "My brothers talk about you all the time. I'd hate to see anything happen to their friend." He extended his hand.

"Thanks," I said.

I watched his white truck drive off and climbed the stairs to my place. I took a hot shower, threw extra blankets on the bed, and crawled under them, still trying to shake off the chill.

CHAPTER TWENTY-ONE

I slept late the next morning, then spent an hour cleaning up my apartment. Once I'd put everything back in its place after the debugging rampage from last night, I climbed on a chair and placed a piece of masking tape over the tiny spying device in the fan. My first thought had been to get in the attic and take it out. But I didn't want to tip my hand just yet. Let them think I still thought they were the FBI. They could have their spyglass, but they wouldn't see me.

After I showered, dressed, and ate, I headed outside and around the house to the garage in the back. First thing I needed to do was get a new cell phone. I turned the corner and ran smack into a man that would give a professional wrestler a run for his money. "Oof!" Just like last night.

A smile formed on the man's face. "Are you okay?" he asked politely.

I noticed a shorter, slender man behind him. Both were dressed in dark suits. A sense of déjà vu swept over me. "What do you want?" I asked.

"I'm Special Agent Forbes with the FBI," the smaller guy

said. He flashed a gold badge at me, then waved a hand at his partner. "This is Special Agent White. We'd like a word with you." No guns, just a civil demeanor.

"Yeah, right," I said. "Wasn't last night enough?" I had quickly gone through a range of emotions, from surprise and fear, to downright pissed off. I hoped the last wouldn't get me killed.

"What do you mean?" Forbes asked.

"Let me see that badge again," I said. He handed it over and I scrutinized it carefully. "How do I know you're who you say you are?" Even as I said it, I noticed a gray sedan with government plates parked down the alley. Government plates – white plates. Not like the dark plates on the SUV last night.

"What happened last night?" A look of genuine puzzlement spread across his face.

"Someone's impersonating you guys."

Forbes and White exchanged a cautious look. "Who might that have been?" Forbes said a bit too lightly.

"Oh, come on," I snapped. "We all know who it was, or you wouldn't be here."

Forbes shrugged. "The X Women, no doubt." He met my gaze. "You're correct. We know about them, as well as your investigation." He frowned. "But pretending to be the FBI is new territory for them."

"How do you know about my investigation unless you've been spying on me," I glared at him. "It was you guys who planted the spy camera in my house."

Forbes shook his head. "No, that's the work of the X Women. But we have been tracking your investigation."

"I feel so exposed." That got a trace of a smile from White.

"What did they do to you?" I briefly explained about my trip in the SUV last night. "It sounds like you must be a threat to them," Forbes mused when I'd finished. "And I wouldn't take that lightly."

"So I gathered," I said.

"Unfortunately, you're a threat to our investigation as well." Forbes stared at me.

"This sounds familiar."

"I need to ask you to stop," Forbes said. "We've been working this case for too long to have the X Women bolt because of the meddling of an amateur detective."

"Amateur? I've done pretty darn well, if I do say so myself."

Forbes was not amused. "You're coming dangerously close to tampering with a federal investigation, Mr. Ferguson. If you do cross the line, I can prosecute you."

"More threats."

White stepped up. "Watch yourself." His nostrils flared. Forbes held him back.

"Leave this to the professionals," Forbes said. They both turned and walked down to the sedan.

I waited until the car disappeared before I let out a deep breath. Threatened by the X Women, and now the real FBI.

I strolled to the garage and pulled the 4-Runner out and drove down the alley. As I turned onto 18th, another sedan pull up behind me. A man in a dark suit and equally dark sunglasses sat behind the wheel. I then saw Special Agent White in the passenger seat. They stayed close to me all the way to the office. The FBI weren't even bothering being subtle.

The feds followed me as I visited a cell phone store and bought a new phone and had the data uploaded onto it, and they were still with me as I drove to my office.

I parked in my space and tried to walk as nonchalantly as possible to my building, but having Big Brother watching made me uneasy. I entered the building through double glass doors and stepped to the left, then peered out through the glass. The sedan sat across the street in a spot where the agents could watch the doors. The driver inserting something into his ear. So, they weren't responsible for the camera device at the condo, but they were listening here. Cute. I hurried through the first floor halls to a back entrance and peeked out the metal door. A similar vehicle was parked in the alley, and I had no doubt that a similar agent was also watching for me. I eased the door shut and took a deep breath. Special Agent Forbes was not kidding.

Once in my office, I peeled off my coat, chucked it onto a chair and went to my desk. I picked up the phone and checked messages. There were three from Amanda, begging me to call her, and one from Cal. He had more information, call when I could. I had no sooner cradled the phone than it rang.

"Where have you been?" Amanda's breathy voice sounded surprisingly lucid. "Why haven't you returned my calls?"

"Things are," I paused, "complicated."

"I have to talk to you. Please, Reed, you have to help me."

"Okay, but we can't talk over the phone," I cut her off. "Come to my office."

"Why?"

"I need to talk to you in person." I didn't want to tell Amanda anything over the phone.

I heard only silence on the other end. "I'll come down now," she finally said.

"Okay."

I hung up without another word and cursed myself for ever taking the case. Now I had to detach myself from her, or my own family and friends would be in danger. I thought about my game plan while I waited. I turned on my MP3 player and selected a Talking Heads CD, turning it up loud. I figured I had about forty-five minutes before Amanda showed. The phone rang again.

"Reed, I thought you were going to call me."

"Sorry, Cal, I got waylaid last night." Literally. "I need to talk to you."

"And I need to talk to you," Cal said. "Hey, turn that down. I've got more stuff on these X Women. I spent all night on this, and..."

I interrupted him. "I - need - to - call - you - back, okay?" I stretched out my words, emphasizing each word carefully.

He immediately sensed something wrong. "Okay, call me when you get a chance." He hung up, and I listened for a second more. I heard another click, just as I'd expected. At least cell phones were difficult to tap. They could still be overheard, so I was going to have to be careful. Thanks to the FBI, I had few options.

I stepped into the outer office with a pad and pen, sat down on the couch and waited. I made notes on the pad while David Byrne sang through "Swamp Thing", one of my favorite Talking Heads songs. Then I waited some more. The stress of the last few days took over, and time seemed to sit still. I felt myself drifting off.

I was sitting with my feet propped up on a corner of the desk, smoking a cigarette in the dim light. I heard the sound of heels clicking on the floor in the hallway. I pulled my fedora hat low over my eyes as a silhouette appeared on the other side of the hazy glass door. With a flourish, a sultry woman entered the room, danger following her even as she smiled with full red lips.

I awoke with a start almost an hour later when the office door clanged open and Amanda strolled in. She wore a light gray slack suit. Her hair was perfectly coiffed, but her face had a strained look on it. I bounced to my feet.

"Reed, what is..." I waved my hands frantically, cutting her off.

"I'm glad you came over," I said, at the same time handing her the pad with my notes. "We need to talk about the case."

"I see," she said, reading the note. On the pad I'd written: "FBI listening act normal. I'll explain."

"I've had a chance to think things through, and I'm not going to pursue this anymore."

Her eyes blinked in confusion. I could tell she didn't know what to believe. "I need your help," she said. "Please don't do this to me."

"I'm sorry," I said, taking the pad back from her. I scribbled on it "I'll explain outside," and handed it back to her.

"Reed, please," she said, looking at the pad. I jerked my head toward the door.

"Why don't I walk you to the elevator?" I touched her elbow, guiding her out. "I need to return your retainer, minus my expenses. I've got an itemized bill, and I wrote you a check for it."

By now we were out the door. I closed it loudly.

She spun on me. "What the hell is going on?"

I placed a finger to my lips and pushed her down the hallway, talking fast as I moved her along. "Look, the FBI knows all about you. They've been following you, me, and who knows who else. They've got my office bugged, and I'm sure they have your house bugged as well. They told me to stop my investigation or they would prosecute me. On top of that, last night the X Women paid me a visit. They've threatened not only me, but my family and friends if I help you anymore. I can't risk that." She slowed down, but I kept steering her forward. "I shouldn't be telling you any of this, and I can't let the FBI know I did."

She twisted away from me. "Wait, Reed. I've got to talk to you. They've contacted me again."

"The X Women?"

"Yes. They want me to meet them in Castle Rock at a restaurant called The Snake Pit, tonight at seven. They know something's going on. I have to go, or they'll kill me. I know they will. But I'm scared. What do they want from me?" Tears welled up in her eyes.

I stared at her. "I can't help you."

She nodded her head vigorously. "Yes, you can. You're the only one who can." She gripped my arm tightly.

I hung my head for a second. The current of this case was sucking me under. "Call me in an hour at this number." I wrote my cell phone number down, ripped off the sheet, and handed it to her. Pressing the elevator button, I said, "Call from a pay phone. Go to the mall or somewhere where there are a lot of people. Make it hard for the feds to keep their eyes on you." The elevator dinged and the doors slid open.

Amanda stepped onto it, holding her hand out to block the doors. "You've got to help me."

"You're in a lot of trouble. You know that, don't you? The feds know that you hired the X Women. They'll arrest you."

Her lips quivered. "That's better than being killed. And the FBI can't keep me from getting killed. You can." She took her hands away and the elevator doors slid shut.

"I doubt it," I whispered to my reflection in the doors.

I returned to the office, grabbed my cell phone, and sprinted back into the hall. No one was to be seen in either direction. I passed by the elevators again and the windows that faced the street. The sedan hadn't moved. At the end of a side hall, a large window opened onto a metal fire escape on one side of the building. I pushed the window open and climbed onto the little platform, then dialed the number. In the alley below, nothing seemed out of the ordinary. Only the sound of traffic on the streets nearby. I chose a number from the cell phone memory and called Cal on his cell phone.

"Why this number?" he asked when I said hello.

"I'm hot," I said. "We've got company listening in at my office and probably at home."

She swore.

"You said it." I quickly explained everything that had transpired. "Those guys last night threatened to expose you if I don't stay out of this thing, and I'm sure they can do it."

"They're threatening me, huh?"

"I'm sorry."

Cal grunted. "Jerks. But I'm smarter than they are." I believed that, but still worried about him.

"She's still in trouble," I said.

"I figured that." A pause. "So you bring her in and let the feds prosecute her. Is that what you're going to do?"

"Can I let her die?"

"You? No. You wouldn't do that."

I took a deep breath of the brisk morning air.

"You're in big trouble, pal. You sure you want to do this?" Cal asked.

"No."

"What do you need from me?"

"I don't know yet, but I'll call you when I need you."

"Watch your back."

"You too," I said and hung up. I hurried back to the office and turned off the music. I grabbed my coat and ran to my car. I had a while before Amanda called, so I drove around, mulling over my situation and letting the FBI guys waste gas tailing me. As I drove, a plan formed in my mind. I was headed west, so I circled the block and drove to St. Joseph's Hospital. I parked in a metered space and dashed across the street, laughing because

I'd taken the last available space. The sedan passed me and turned the corner.

The emergency room doors slid open, Star-Trek style, and Willie looked up from behind the admissions desk. "What brings you here?" she said with a smile, her green eyes dancing. "Do you have an emergency?"

I nodded, sat down, and explained what I needed from her. Inside of five minutes, I was back in the 4-Runner. The FBI vehicle was double-parked near mine. I waved at the agents and peeled off. They followed me to City Park, where I pulled into a space and waited for a phone call. The sedan pulled in across the street, the agents clearly watching me.

My cell phone rang twenty minutes later. I peeled out of my parking space, putting distance between the sedan and me.

"I'm at a pay phone at the Cherry Creek Mall," Amanda said.

"Be ready at six," I said.

"What are you going to do?"

"I'll come through the back yard. Don't say anything. Leave some loud music on in your living room."

"Music?"

"To help muffle any sounds. And stay sober."

"Reed," she said.

"Just do it. Okay?"

"Okay."

I hung up and drove back to the office. I suddenly had a lot of work to do.

CHAPTER TWENTY-TWO

"All right, I don't see anyone." I was standing at the edge of Amanda Ghering's back yard, scanning the perimeter of her property with night-vision goggles purchased earlier in the day from an Army surplus store. I had no way of knowing if the feds had Amanda's house surrounded or if they only had a car out front. Or did they have someone watching at all? I had come prepared. But after a careful look around, I didn't see anyone. Just houses, trees, and an occasional fence, all neon green from the goggles. "Let's go," I whispered.

"This is exciting," Willie whispered back as she followed me. She looked really cute in black slacks and sweater and a heavy navy blue jacket, her short blond hair tucked into a Rockies baseball cap. "My life needed more adventure."

"Shh," I hissed. We'd made it this far unseen, and I wanted to keep it that way.

A couple of hours earlier, I'd gone with the Goofball Brothers to B 52's. Thursday nights there are fairly crowded. I started a game of pool with the brothers, then left them there and managed to lose my FBI tail by sneaking out the back, where Willie had been waiting with her car in the alley. Forty minutes later, we had arrived at Amanda's house.

We ran in a crouch up to the back porch. I took a quick look behind us, but didn't notice anything. No dogs barking, no people in their yards. Music drifted out to us. I tapped quietly on the rear door. Nothing. I rapped a little harder and the door opened. Beethoven's Fifth Symphony blared out.

I put my hand up to my lips. Amanda, decked out in red designer jeans and white sweater, gestured for us to come in the house. The back door led into a darkened kitchen, the white walls and cabinets glowing eerily from an overhead light in the front entryway. On the gray granite countertop next to the sink were a blond wig and a long fur overcoat with a high collar. Willie took off her cap and donned the wig, peeled off her own coat, then shrugged into Amanda's fur coat. I fixed the collar, pulling it up around her ears. I turned her to the side, sizing up the disguise.

I mouthed "perfect" to her. She smiled, kissed me lightly on the cheek, and took the car keys that Amanda offered her. Amanda led the way to the garage, and Willie tiptoed out in the dark. She got in the Lexus and waited for my signal. Amanda strolled into the living room, shut off the stereo, slipped into a black leather jacket, and came back to join me. I signaled to Willie. As I shut the inner door, she opened the garage door. Amidst the rumble from the automatic door opener, Amanda and I tiptoed out the back door.

We sidled up to the side of the house, just in time to see the Lexus turn out of the driveway. Willie was doing her job well. It was impossible to tell who was driving the car. In a few seconds, a dark sedan drove down the street after Amanda's Lexus. The feds were watching, and they bought our ruse. I turned around and gave Amanda a thumbs-up sign.

I took a moment to scan the yard with the field glasses. All clear. Amanda and I grabbed hands, bent low, and ran for the edge of the yard. We reached a tall pine tree. I pulled us around it and stopped. We were both breathing hard.

"I think we fooled them," I whispered. "But we don't have much time."

"Where is she going?"

"I don't know. She'll drive around, get a burger or something and head back."

"I would never do that. Especially just to get a burger. Yuck!" Amanda made a gagging motion with her finger in her mouth.

"It doesn't matter, as long as she keeps the FBI away from us." I leaned close to her, smelling her breath. "Have you been drinking?"

"I needed something to calm my nerves."

I glared at her. "I told you not to drink. If one thing goes wrong..." The sentence hung in the air. If one thing did go wrong, I would be getting a lot of people in trouble.

"Come on." I climbed the waist-high chain-link fence, helped Amanda over, and ran off through her neighbor's yard, over to the next street. We ran two long blocks, past huge houses, heading east.

"Wait," Amanda halted abruptly.

"What?" I said, gasping for breath.

"I have to pee." She looked miserable.

"What?"

"I'm nervous, and I have to go."

I threw up my hands in exasperation. "Hold it." I started running again.

"I can't."

"Well," I smiled sweetly. "You have plenty of choice trees and bushes."

She gave me a withering look and stalked off between two

151

houses. I prayed no one would choose this moment to look out their windows. In two minutes she was back, looking relieved.

"Come on!" I said.

"You don't need to get so mad," she said, dashing after me.

"We're in a hurry." We ran for three more blocks.

"Wait," she called out again.

"What?" My patience was wearing thin.

"This running is hurting my feet."

"You shouldn't have worn heels," I said, pointing at her spiked pumps. "And what's with the red? When I called this afternoon I said to dress in dark clothes."

"I have to look good for my meeting," she said with a pout.

"Right, I'm sure it's important to make a good impression now."

She gave me another scornful look. "That's not funny."

"Come on, we're wasting time." One more block up I spied a beat-up Honda Civic. I sprinted to it and opened the passenger door. I flipped up the seat and clambered into the back. "Get in," I ordered Amanda, who stood looking at the car in surprise.

"I wondered how you were getting me to the restaurant," she said as she sat down in the front seat.

"This is Cal," I introduced him as he pulled away from the curb.

"Where to?" Cal asked, barely acknowledging Amanda. I directed him to The Snake Pit, a restaurant in Castle Rock, where Amanda's rendezvous was taking place.

"So you're Reed's help?" Amanda said, placing well-manicured fingers on Cal's arm.

If Cal knew she was flirting with him, he didn't show it. He kept his eyes on the road, and Amanda removed her hand and stared out the window. She had no idea how I had to cajole Cal into helping me. Unlike Willie, he wasn't interested in the adventure, and even my undying friendship didn't sway him. This was a man who rarely ventured from his house, had his groceries delivered, and did most of his shopping over the Internet. The outside world held no interest for him. But when I mentioned the FBI, he changed his mind. I don't think he liked being threatened by them.

"So what's with the Navy Seal look?" Cal asked, looking at me in the rear view mirror. I had dressed completely in black: jeans, sweatshirt, socks, shoes, and knit cap pulled low over my ears. At least I hadn't painted my face black.

"I didn't want anyone to see us," I said, reaching around the seat and poking Amanda in the ribs.

"My jacket's black, and so are my heels." She crossed her arms and tossed her hair at me. I met Cal's gaze in the mirror. His brown eyes sparkled with humor.

We drove the rest of the way in silence. I kept peering out the back window, but never saw a car tailing us. Apparently we had given the FBI the slip. That made twice for me. And no one would pay attention to Cal's beat-up Honda.

At five minutes to seven Cal drove past The Snake Pit. It was a small, family-run restaurant stuck in between a used bookstore and a liquor store. Three big bay windows faced the street, with an entrance to the right of them. Cal turned the corner and parked the Civic on a side street a block from the restaurant.

Amanda turned around. "All right," I said. "Find out what they want. Don't do anything you wouldn't normally do. And don't drink."

"But that's what I would normally do," she said.

"True," I acknowledged. "But I need you sober so you can keep everything straight. I want a detailed description of who meets you, what she, or he, says. And what the X Women want.

Sit at a table near the windows if you can, so I can see who meets you. Got it?"

She bobbed her head up and down. "Where will you be?"

"I'll see if I can watch from outside somewhere. And I'll meet you back here." She opened the door and got out. I followed her, and waited while she walked to the corner. Then she disappeared from view.

"If anything happens, meet me at that gas station," I said and pointed to a Conoco down the road. "I don't know how long this'll take."

"Go," Cal ordered as I slammed the door shut.

I jogged to the corner and stuck my head around the building. Amanda had reached the restaurant, and a valet was holding the restaurant door for her. I counted to sixty, but didn't see anyone enter behind her. I crossed the street and walked down the block, stopping at the street corner. A couple came out of the restaurant and handed a ticket to the valet. He dashed off down the street to retrieve their car, and I took the opportunity to walk back to a store directly across from The Snake Pit. I stepped back into the shadows of the entrance and watched.

I couldn't see Amanda in the restaurant. I was disappointed to see that the three available window tables were occupied. I checked my watch. Five after seven. The valet came back with the car and the couple drove off. A group of four came from the direction where Cal was waiting. They walked casually inside. I leaned out to get a better view down the street and froze.

At the same corner I had just occupied was a woman in a long tan overcoat and dark hat whose floppy brim obscured her face. She looked left and right, waited for a white minivan to pass, then crossed the street and entered the restaurant. I didn't think she'd seen me. And I hadn't seen her face, but I'd bet my Navy Seal cap she was an X Woman.

I didn't think it'd be long now. I looked at my watch again. Seven ten. I squinted but couldn't see anything beyond people dining at the tables near the windows. Watching them eat was making me hungry. My stomach growled. I reached in my pocket for a Snickers bar and unwrapped it as quietly as I could. I was probably breaking every rule of undercover work, but I'd been so nervous I hadn't eaten since this morning. I needed the extra energy, I told myself.

I bit off half the candy bar and almost moaned, it tasted so good right then. I was so engrossed in my candy bar that I almost missed the woman in the tan overcoat coming back across the street. I swallowed hard and nearly gagged on peanuts, nougat, and chocolate.

I stopped chewing and held my breath until she passed by. I took a hesitant step forward and looked to the right. She was gone. I looked back at the The Snake Pit. Amanda had just come out the door and was walking hurriedly back toward the car. I followed on the other side of the street, guiltily finishing the Snickers. Once Amanda turned down the side street where Cal was parked, I started running. She swirled around when she was about ten feet from the car, her face tight with fear, then relief when she recognized me.

"They want another meeting," she said as we slid into the car.

"That was quick," Cal said. He'd left the car running and without delay he made a u-turn and we started back to Amanda's house.

"They want another meeting?" I repeated. "What for?"

Amanda arched her eyebrows at me. "How should I know? They want to meet again in two days. I'm supposed to call from a pay phone tomorrow morning at eleven-thirty to receive instructions. That's exactly what she said: *receive instructions*.

How silly can they make this?" Amanda's voice dripped derision.

"What else did she say?"

"How did you know it was a woman?"

"The X *Women?*" Cal said.

"The woman in the tan overcoat and hat," I said. "It was her, right?"

"Yes. She sat down at the table, ordered a white wine spritzer, and told me that I'd complicated things. They needed my help to straighten everything out. I asked about Peter, and she said someone would explain everything to me at the next meeting. She said not to talk to anyone, and that they'll inform me tomorrow about where the next meeting will be. Then she left."

"Before she had her drink?" Cal asked. "How rude."

I punched his arm. "Quit it." I focused on Amanda. "That's it? Nothing else?" She shook her head. "What's the point of all this?" she said angrily. "Why not tell me now instead of dragging me through all this?"

"Onion skins," Cal said.

"What's that supposed to mean?"

I explained about Cal's analogy of putting layers between each person in the organization, so no one person knows too much about what the other members are doing.

"What did she look like?" I asked Amanda.

She bit her lower lip while she thought. "A little tall, although she did have on heels. She had brown hair, cut in a bob. It didn't look good on her, either. And she needed more makeup. Her face isn't attractive enough to skimp on that. No earrings either."

I caught Cal rolling his eyes in the rear view mirror.

"Amanda?" I asked.

"Yes?"

"Do you have anything more than fashion observations?"

"I'm just trying to tell you what I saw," she said. "She wasn't very attractive."

"What color were her eyes? Did she look like she had a gun or anything? Did she talk with an accent or do anything that would give away where she was from?"

"Blue, no, and no."

"So she was an ordinary woman, maybe a little tall, with brown hair."

"And unattractive," Cal added.

Amanda agreed. "I don't see how this is helping anything."

I sat back, right on my impulse to say something sarcastic. I pulled my cell phone out and dialed Willie's number. By now we were back on I-25.

"Who're you calling?" Amanda asked.

"Willie. I need to tell her to head back to your house now."

"Where is she?" Amanda asked.

I held up a hand for silence. "Done," I said into the phone.

"Half hour," Willie said to me, then hung up.

I pocketed the cell phone. "She'll be there in a half hour. She'll let herself in and wait for us. Her instructions are to turn the stereo back on again and wait in the kitchen."

"You have this all planned out, don't you?" Amanda said, reappraising me.

"It wasn't easy." I thought back to the number of trips I took to the fire escape or the bathroom on the main floor of my building so I could call Willie or Cal on the cell phone. And apparently no FBI types heard, because this was going off without a hitch.

"Here we are," Cal interrupted us. We were back on the same street where he'd picked us up. Amanda and I got out.

"I'll be back," I said, in my best Arnold Schwarzenegger voice. I shut the door and Amanda and I ran down the street, retracing our steps from earlier in the evening. The moon was out now, casting everything in shadows.

A sudden beep pierced the quiet. I stopped cold and Amanda plowed into me.

"Oh, no. We're dead," she gasped, holding a hand up to her neck.

I heard my heart beating in my ears, and then the beep again. I shook my head. "It's only my cell phone." I extracted it with shaky hands from my coat pocket before it could beep again. "What?" I murmured into the phone. A second passed before I thrust the phone at Amanda. "It's Willie. She set off the burglar alarm! Quick! Tell her what to do."

"Oh, is that all?" Amanda took the phone from me, told Willie how to turn off the alarm, then handed it back to me. "See? No big deal."

"Are you trying to sabotage this?" I nearly exploded. "I damn near crapped my pants."

"Well, I did, if it makes you happy." She put her hands defiantly on her hips.

I got in her face. "Why the hell did you set the burglar alarm in the first place?"

"If you didn't want me to, you should've asked. You were standing right by the back door with me. And keep your voice down."

"I had a few other things on my mind." And I did now too, like maybe I should take her out myself and save the X Women the trouble. "Hurry up."

In ten minutes, we were back in Amanda's kitchen, a rock station blaring from the stereo in the living room. Willie reluctantly gave back the fur coat and put on her Rockies cap. I wrote on a pad for Amanda to call me on my cell the next day at noon. Then Willie and I slipped out into the darkness, leaving Amanda to her vodka and her bathroom facilities.

CHAPTER TWENTY-THREE

"They left you in the middle of nowhere?" Cal said, thumping his bottle of beer angrily on the table. We'd dropped Willie off in the alley behind her apartment and watched her sneak through her back yard and in the back door. Once she signaled that everything was okay, Cal and I went for a beer at The Punch Bowl, a small bar near my place. We fought the late-night crowd and found a table at the back. Once seated, I told Cal about my adventures the previous night, the first chance I'd had to talk without fear of the X Women or the FBI listening in. "I thought that kind of stuff only happened in the movies."

"Yeah, so did I." I took a long sip on my beer. I couldn't concentrate on what he was saying. I kept thinking about the rendezvous at the restaurant. Amanda had the X Women worried. They'd broken their own rules, meeting with her. The X Women didn't make contact after the wheels started into motion, that's what Amanda and Maggie had both said. More meetings exposed them to even greater risk. But now they wanted another meeting. I could see why Amanda was so scared. The X Women meant to deal with her. But how? And

159

what had happened to Peter? Did his fate, whatever it was, somehow make her more of a liability, or less?

"Are you listening to me?"

"Sorry," I said. "This whole thing is a mess. It doesn't make sense. And Peter's probably dead."

"Amanda doesn't care about him. You know that, don't you?"

I nodded slowly. "The X Women probably want to kill her, too. That worries me."

"Even though she nearly ruined it for you tonight with that burglar alarm?" Cal asked.

"Amanda can help us figure out what happened to Peter."

"How?"

"By getting closer to the X Women. She goes to the meeting, where she asks what happened to him."

"Maybe they just want to kill her," Cal voiced my concern. "Do you know how easy it would be for the X Women to kidnap her? They can eliminate her so fast the FBI, or you, would never even know it."

I finished my beer. "I can't let that happen. She deserves jail, but not death."

"You're probably the only detective who's ever helped the guilty person." Cal raised his beer bottle in a toast.

"Just like the movies." I signaled to the waitress and ordered another beer. "Humphrey Bogart helped some pretty shaky heroines."

"You're not Bogie."

I forced a smile. "No kidding."

We talked for a while longer and then Cal took me home.

"You want me to drive back down the alley?" Cal asked as we turned near my neighborhood.

I started to nod my head. "No, wait. Drop me off in front."

Cal turned his head. "They'll know you ditched them."

"I know. Serves them right for watching us."

Cal turned down my street and pulled in front of my building, his headlights illuminating the FBI vehicle right in front of us. I got out of Cal's car and walked around the front. Agent White's eyes widened in surprise. I waved at him. He glowered back at me as he pulled out a cell phone. I turned and grinned at Cal, who laughed as he drove off. Tapping the hood of the sedan, I said, "Better luck next time." White yelled something at me as I climbed up the side stairs, but it didn't bother me. I crawled into bed and was asleep within ten minutes.

———

At twenty minutes to twelve the next day, I took a walk into downtown Denver, presumably to visit the bank. What I really needed was a noisy, crowded place where I could take Amanda's call, someplace where it would be difficult for the feds to listen in.

One of the benefits of living in Colorado is the rapid temperature changes. On any day, the weather can swing from freezing cold to sunny skies and soothing warmth. This was such a day, and I walked in the spring-like weather, enjoying the bright blue skies and temperatures in the upper 50's. People lucky enough to have Friday off left their coats and gloves behind as they strolled toward restaurants on the Sixteenth Street Mall for lunch. Birds chirped from bare branches. And now, two FBI agents tailed me.

Agent White, who seemed exceedingly unhappy when I greeted him, stayed in his car, crawling down the streets behind me. His new partner, a tall, emaciated-looking fellow, kept pace with me, leaving about thirty feet between us as we walked. At least if I got mugged I would have a witness or two, although I doubt Agent White or his partner would bother to help me.

At noon, I was standing in the lobby of Wells Fargo at 17th

and Curtis, filling out a withdrawal slip, when my cell phone rang. As I answered it, I glanced out the smoky glass windows onto 17th. The black sedan was parked on the street, just outside the entrance to the building. My walking companion stood outside the bank entrance, watching me through the glass doors.

"It's me," Amanda said. "The message came through."

"What's the next move?" I turned to face the teller windows, leaning away from the doors where the skinny agent watched me.

"I'm supposed to meet them at P.F. Chang's at Park Meadows Mall. Monday night at seven."

"Them? There's more than one?"

"That's what they said."

"They? Who did you talk to?"

"It was a distorted voice, the same as before. I don't know if it was a him, her, or them, okay?"

She knew how to try a person's patience. "What happens then?" I asked.

"It," she said caustically, "didn't say. I'm to ask for the reservation for M-O-R-T-E." She spelled it for me.

"Interesting," I said. I used the reflection in my sunglasses to keep an eye on the doors. So far, the skinny guy didn't seem overly interested in what I was doing.

"What do I do?"

"Meet them."

"Reed," Amanda said. "What are you going to do?"

I stared at the deposit slip, my mind as blank as the balance on the paper. "Sit tight. I'll work out a plan and call you when I've got something."

"When?" she persisted.

"Give me twenty-four hours. I'll call you on your cell phone." I hung up and stood at the little table with the deposit and withdrawal forms, feeling I'd been deposited, right in a pile of crap. I didn't know much about the X Women, but this was weird.

To keep up pretenses, I finished filling out the form, visited a teller and withdrew some cash. As I walked out of the bank I passed the gaunt agent who now leaned against the marble wall across from the entrance. I winked at him. He raised one eyebrow at me and waited until I was out on Seventeenth before he followed.

I basked in the sunshine as I strolled back home, pretending that there weren't two feds tracking my every move. I ate a turkey sandwich, and went to the garage for the 4-Runner. I spent the remainder of the day scoping out P.F. Chang's at Park Meadows Mall.

Park Meadows is one of Denver's ritzier shopping malls, a sprawling complex of buildings and restaurants at the junction of I-25 and C-470. P.F. Chang's restaurant, a trendy place serving westernized Chinese food, is situated on the east side of the mall, between two other restaurants.

As I sat in my car, studying the lay of the land, I had to admit the X Women chose the place well. The restaurant was crowded now, at the end of the lunch hour, and I'm sure it would be just as packed at seven tomorrow night. If I planned to kidnap somebody, I would choose a crowded place like this. The lines of parking lanes, stretching all the way back to the mall, would be perfect. The X Women could walk Amanda outside and easily persuade her into a car. There would be so many people, busy doing their own things, so no one would even notice.

I sketched a picture of the layout, then decided to go in for a light snack, leaving Agent White and his companion watching from their vehicle, parked one row from mine. After a ten-minute wait, a frazzled hostess seated me at a table by windows facing south. The atmosphere of the restaurant was very open, with postmodern metal-legged tables and matching chairs. With few walls, the sounds of voices and dishes rattling echoed noisily. Again, a perfect choice. Who would be able to overhear a conversation between a couple of women amidst all the other competing conversations? I could barely hear myself think, and the lunch crowd was diminishing.

A pleasant waiter came over, and I ordered Mongolian beef, extra hot, and an iced tea. I made notes of where the emergency exits were, as well as the restrooms and the kitchen. I still didn't have a plan of what to do, nor did I know if the X Women were going to kidnap Amanda, but having an escape route seemed to be prudent. My Mongolian beef, full of red peppers, arrived. I ate it all with an obscene pleasure and then left.

To make more work for my FBI tails, I decided to wander around the mall for a while. Later in the afternoon, I drove to B-52's, playing pool in an attempt to clear my mind. The two FBI agents came in and had drinks at the bar, presumably soda water, while they surreptitiously watched me play. I was beyond caring. As I shot game after game, I couldn't shake the fact that the X Women were putting themselves in a dangerous situation, and that there was much more to why they were changing their modus operandi. It didn't make sense.

———

By eight o'clock I decided that no matter how much I practiced, I still couldn't hit the two-rail kick shot, where the cue ball hits two rails before hitting the target ball, and I didn't know any more about what the X Women were up to. I won a game playing against a couple of college students, then drove home with my spirits slightly bolstered. As I came up the walk,

Deuce bolted out the front door. He stumbled off the porch stairs and did a 9.6 somersault into the lawn.

"Whoa," I said, helping him to his feet. "What's up there, pardner?"

"Dude," he said, out of breath. "I'm in a hurry."

"No kidding. But you'll end up on your butt again if you're not careful."

"Yeah, but I gotta get this movie back. Ace will kill me if it's late."

"What'd you rent?" He held out a DVD case, which I read. *The Big Sleep*. "So you guys finally rented it. I could've loaned you my copy."

Deuce bobbed his head up and down. "Ace got it for free. He works at the video store, you know."

I nodded knowingly with him. "What'd you think of the movie?"

He scrunched up his nose in distaste. "I didn't get it. All these people get killed, but you don't get to see it, 'cause it all happened some other time. Except at the end of the movie. That guy, Marlowe, was that his name? He fooled them, didn't he? You would think the other guy would know that Marlowe was going to get him. The good guy always wins. Even I know that."

"Ah, that's the best part," I said, clapping him on the shoulder.

I loved that part, my favorite hero, Bogie, outwits the bad guy, Eddie Mars. Bogie sets him up, and then gets Mars to explain all the killings. He causes Mars to be killed by his own gang members, all the loose ends are wrapped up nice and tidy, and Bogie gets the girl in the end.

"Why do you keep talking golf?" He brushed a hand over his hair, seeming frustrated.

"Deuce, you're right. Bogie is a golf term, but it's also the nickname of the actor. Humphrey Bogart plays the main character, Philip Marlowe."

"The guy with the hat."

I nodded uncertainly. After all, there were a lot of guys with hats on in those old movies. I wasn't entirely sure we were talking about the same guy. "Yeah, Bogie wore a hat, and he was the detective. The one who figures it all out. Like me."

"Huh?" Deuce looked more baffled now, not an unusual occurrence.

"Forget it," I said. "Return the movie. Sorry I got in your way." Deuce rolled his eyes at me and sprinted off.

He ran past a dark sedan, where Agent White's replacement sat observing us, and disappeared around the corner. I was my usual friendly self with the new agent, waving a greeting as I walked upstairs to my condo.

CHAPTER TWENTY-FOUR

I didn't sleep well that night. I kept dreaming that I had to rescue Amanda, who resembled a very sexy Lauren Bacall, and I was not unlike Bogie. We were at P.F. Chang's, and an X Woman who looked like Xena, the Warrior Princess, was trying to kidnap Amanda. Right when I'd come in to rescue her, my father would show up and ask when I was going to get a real job, while my mother stood beside him asking if I was smoking marijuana. I awoke with a start at dawn. After ten minutes of staring at the ceiling, I decided it was a good time for a run.

The morning was crisp and clear as I came down the steps and around the corner. Ace was exiting his placc, a steaming coffee mug in his hand.

"What're you doing working so early on a Saturday?" I asked him. I rarely saw Ace before nine or ten because he worked odd hours at the video store, usually late nights, not mornings. And never this early.

"I told Bob I'd help him work on his truck," Ace said. I noticed now that the jeans he wore were torn and smudged with grease.

"I hear you didn't like the movie." I was doing all I could to avoid my run.

He grimaced. "Sorry, man. I didn't get it. Trying to follow who killed who. At least with Arnold Schwarzenegger you know who gets killed. And didn't that guy Mars know that the detective was going to get him in the end? Mars should've known that. The good guy always wins. Arnold always wins."

"I'll be sure to tell Bogie that."

"Huh?"

"Never mind," I said, waving him off. I noticed my FBI tail was there, with two bleary-eyed agents sitting in the front seat. They looked desperate to get off duty.

I did some stretching on the front porch, cracked my neck, and retied my shoes. After that I couldn't find any more excuses, so I took off in a sprint, determined to run at least five miles. Okay, maybe three.

As I ran, my mind wandered over things. Carmen, the femme fatale in *The Big Sleep*, reminded me of Amanda. Both were sneaky, seductive, and ultimately fallen. I doubted Amanda would appreciate the comparison. And it didn't surprise me that the Brothers had a hard time following the movie. There were seven murders, and most of them happened off-screen. I thought the brothers might like the shootout at the end, though. Bogie fools the crooks, and gets Mars to walk right into his own trap.

And then it hit me. I couldn't believe the Goofball Brothers saw it and I didn't. I stopped, turned around, and ran like Eddie Mars was after me, all the way home.

I took the porch steps two at a time and ran headlong up the stairs. I used my cell phone to call Cal to discuss my theory, thinking we could talk in some kind of code so my FBI listeners wouldn't know what we were really saying. But I got his answering machine, so I left a message to call me as soon as he could. Since he rarely left his house, he had to be in the shower. At least that's what I hoped. He would call soon.

I hung up the phone and found my copy of *The Big Sleep* sitting on the shelf with my other favorite movies. I pulled it out of the case as I walked into the living room. I slid in the DVD and sat down on the edge of the couch with the remote control aimed like a gun at the player.

The Big Sleep. The title referred to death, to villains doing evil deeds while the city sleeps and when some fool gets in the way, he's killed. I watched Bogie and Bacall in their first scene together. Did they ever create some intense chemistry. It was just getting to the good stuff, Bacall at her seductive best, when the phone rang.

I paused the movie and grabbed the cordless phone sitting on the end table. "It's about time."

"About time for what, dear?"

"Oh. Hi Mom," I said.

"Don't sound so disappointed, dear," she said.

"I'm kind of busy right now."

"You should never be too busy for your mother, darling, and don't get fresh with me. You sound better than you did the other night. I was worried about you, but your father said to leave you alone. You're a man now, and I needn't worry myself over you, even if you do such silly things and put yourself in danger. Were you in danger, dear? It wasn't drugs, was it?" She was on a roll. If I didn't know better, I'd say *she* was the one on drugs.

"If you only knew," I said in exasperation.

"Yes, we're fine. You sound funny. What're you doing? Are you okay?" She was off and running, asking me about the job, did I get the oranges, and telling me that I should choose a less dangerous profession. I heard my father in the background, yelling something about me being an adult and making my own decisions, even if they weren't the brightest. "Anyway, dear," Mom rushed to wrap up the conversation. "I'm excited to see you. You have all our flight information."

I assured her I did.

"Okay, darling. I must be going." I said I'd see her soon. "Oh, and Reed?" She rarely called me by my first name. "Yes?" I was all ears. "Do be careful." She paused. "I love you, dear."

So that was the heart of the call. She was more than a little worried after our talk the other night. I made a mental note to shield her from the dangerous aspects of my new profession. And to tell her that I loved her, which I did.

I focused on the DVD again, trying to find the scene that I was searching for, where Marlowe, played by Bogie, kills the villain, Mars. I thought this would answer the question about how the X Women wanted to deal with Amanda. Just like Ace had mentioned, the bad guy can't outwit the good guy.

After scanning scenes for a bit, I found the part I wanted near the end, where Marlowe sets up Mars. Marlowe has arranged a meeting with Mars, but Marlowe arrives much earlier than the appointed time. Now he only has to wait.

Mars arrives at the meeting place early, planning to have his henchmen hide outside and ambush Marlowe. But Mars, of course, has no idea that Marlowe is already there.

I sat back on the couch, watching the black-and-white scene unfold, the remote dangling in my hand. The setup: The X Women were playing with Amanda, making her run around in circles, confusing her, the same way Marlowe put one over on Mars in the movie, distracting her with instructions about the supposed rendezvous. It reminded me of how Mars and Marlowe each tried to get the jump on the other one in the lead-up to that climactic scene in the movie. Amanda would be so focused on the meeting tomorrow night that she, and her detective helper – me - wouldn't be expecting anything between now and then. The X Women would be way ahead of us. I watched Bogie and Bacall, smoking in the dark as the movie ended, but my mind wasn't on them.

Amanda and I were in trouble. The meeting tomorrow night was a decoy, I was sure of it. Whatever was going to happen, would happen before then. The X Women were setting us up, just like Mars planned to ambush Marlowe by striking before he expected it. The question was, could Amanda and I beat them at their own "set-up" game the way Marlowe outwitted Mars?

I paced in the living room for a minute, not sure what to do. Should I call Amanda and tell her, knowing the FBI was listening in? What if I was wrong? I'd look like an idiot, and I would've tipped my hand about the meeting tomorrow. And I would anger Agent Forbes because I remained involved. I didn't want that. But what if I was right? I tried Cal again, wanting to use him as a sounding board.

I decided the first thing to do was to get out of my sweaty running clothes, so I peeled them off, showered and dressed in jeans and black turtleneck. By the time I'd finished, I had determined that I would talk to Amanda. I would deal with the FBI consequences later. I left another message for Cal to call me on my cell phone, grabbed my car keys and ran out of the house. In ten minutes, I was fighting mid-morning traffic and road construction on my way to Amanda's house. I barely noticed Agent White trying to keep up with me as I sped around cars and semis, my concern for Amanda's safety growing. I needed to get to her before it was too late.

I turned off the highway, skidding on gravel. I corrected the 4-Runner and careened around the winding roads to Amanda's house. I pulled into the driveway and ran up to the door. I didn't care if the FBI knew. I needed to get Amanda out, and I didn't care what it did to Agent Forbes' investigation. He'd probably wait until he had something to nail the X Women with before he did anything. And I had a hunch that would probably be too late.

I punched the doorbell and heard the chimes ring hollowly inside. I waited a few seconds, then jammed the button again. Nothing. I stepped off the porch and looked into the living room. I tried to peek between the blinds, but couldn't see anything. I trotted back to the 4-Runner and looked at the house windows for any signs of life. If Amanda was home, she was sleeping like the dead. I hoped it wasn't more than that. I backed out of the driveway and drove on down the street, but didn't notice any sign of her FBI tails. So she wasn't home.

I drove to the club vaguely aware that Agent White was not behind me anymore. I must've lost him somewhere on the way to Amanda's house. I wondered if he was aware of Amanda's lunch routine. I passed by the valet and parked the car myself.

I hurried inside, ignoring the receptionist, who called after me as I ran down the hallway to the bar. I saw Maggie Delacroix sitting in a booth by the entrance. Her eyes widened in a hint of recognition and maybe surprise, before she casually resumed her lunch. I walked past her and saw Amanda, who sat at a corner table in semi-darkness, her chin resting on her hands. She was oblivious to anything going on around her. She didn't even notice me standing by her table.

"You need to come with me," I said in a low voice.

She jumped. "Oh, you startled me." She picked up her glass and tossed back the rest of the drink. "Do you want something?"

I bent down and whispered in her ear. "I think you're being set up. I don't think tomorrow's meeting is ever supposed to happen. Whatever's going to happen, it's going to happen before then."

"Oh, Reed, don't be absurd." Amanda shifted in her chair

and trained unfocused eyes on me. "Did you get this idea from one of your movies? Or a how-to manual?"

"I'm trying to help you," I said through gritted teeth. "If you want, I'll walk away and leave you to figure this out."

"You have to admit that you're a rank amateur," Amanda said with a restrained laugh.

"You're already drunk," I said.

She wagged her head slowly. "No, I'm just feeling really good." She worked hard to enunciate her words. "I am not drunk. But you," she cocked a finger at me, "need to relax. Get a drink, that'll help. Then we can talk about these silly X Women. Come on, sit down now. I'm sorry if I hurt your feelings." She patted the seat of the chair next to her.

"Amanda," I hissed. "Let's get out of here. We can talk about this somewhere else. Somewhere safe."

"I'm perfectly safe here." Amanda stood up. "But I do need to go to the ladies room." She swayed momentarily as she stepped around me and began to walk purposefully out of the bar. "This is a private club. Nothing's going to happen here," she called a little too loudly over her shoulder.

I shrugged at the curious bartender and followed Amanda. She stalked around the corner, down the hall and past the receptionist, who began her protestations about me again. Amanda shooed her back to her desk and disappeared through the bathroom door. I paced the hallway near the door, waiting for her. A minute later a woman in a red dress walked down the hall toward the ladies room. I started to say something to her, I don't even know what, but she froze me with a steely gaze.

"Do you have a problem if I use the restroom?" Her voice was husky, and her eyes flashed at me.

"No," I murmured, turning away from the door. I felt my ears and face burning. After a second I glanced over my shoulder. The door was shutting. I paced again, my impatience growing. A few minutes later the door opened and the woman emerged. She gave me another icy glare and walked away. I waited until she was gone and then I cracked the door open.

"Amanda?"

"Can't a woman go to the bathroom in peace?" Amanda said as she came around a tiled wall. "I'm finished, thank you."

"I was worried," I explained, holding the door open for her.

She bumped past me and turned toward the bar. "Oh no." I steered her in the opposite direction. "I've got to get you out of here. You can drink somewhere else."

"Reed," she said, pulling away from me. "This is absurd."

"You wouldn't think so if you were sober. Come on."

She looked at me with a hurt expression. "You can be so mean." I concurred as I steered her away from the main entrance, continuing down the hall. "Let's find another way out of here," I said soothingly. She seemed to be walking better now, not quite so drunk.

"There's an exit this way. Out back." Amanda jerked her arm away from me, and stalked ahead of me. "You had better have some good vodka where we're going."

I thought about taking her to a detox center, but I didn't want to subject her to anyone else. "You're not making this easy," I said.

"Whatever." By now we had turned a corner and come to an exit. She pushed the door with her shoulder. The door suddenly opened wide and Amanda stumbled forward. The woman in the red dress stood in the opening, one hand on the door. Another tall woman in blue jeans and checked blazer stood behind her. Red Dress grabbed Amanda and pulled her toward Blazer Girl, who placed a white rag over Amanda's nose and mouth. Amanda flailed her arms for a second before going limp. Another woman emerged from a blue van parked at the curb, and helped hustle Amanda into the back of the van. That was all I noticed, because a fourth, surly-looking woman put her round mug into my face and wrapped me in a bear hug, pinning my arms to my sides. Then Red Dress, who was much stronger than she looked, covered my face with a rag. It smelled like chloroform. I gurgled out a cry for help, but it came out a muffled "ugh". I was vaguely aware of Red Dress saying something to me before my vision blurred and I was shoved into the van. Then I saw darkness.

CHAPTER TWENTY-FIVE

A piercing pain in my elbow brought me back to reality. I felt cold on my right cheek. I jerked up, banging my head on a seat. I struggled into a sitting position, swaying with the motion of the van. Amanda was slumped over on the seat near me. She must've gotten a heavier dose of chloroform. That, or she'd finally passed out from all the alcohol in her system. Blazer Girl sat next to her with a look of total indifference on her face. I reached up toward Amanda.

"Don't move," said a voice from the front seat. I turned that way, and ended up staring right into the end of a revolver. "If you do, I'll be forced to use this."

I sat back into the cramped corner between the seat and the van wall. Red Dress watched me over the gun. I stared back. The van hit a nasty bump and we were jostled around, but the gun did not waver. "Where are you taking us?" I finally asked.

No one answered. From my sitting position I could see very little, only the occasional telephone pole or the top of a building. I noticed the sky turning cloudy, with hints of blue peeking out. It was impossible to tell how long I'd been out, but judging by the light outside, not much time had passed.

The van made a right turn. I sat up as much as I dared without Red Dress noticing and saw through her window what looked like an industrial park, with long rows of off-white stucco buildings. We turned down an alley between two buildings, and a large garage door opened. The van pulled in, plunging us into darkness. As soon as the engine died, a flurry of activity ensued.

Red Dress and the driver got out. The side door slid open and Blazer Girl hauled Amanda's limp body out, dragging her roughly through a white door ten feet from the van. Blazer Girl reappeared a moment later. Red Dress gestured with the gun for me to get out. I crawled out of the van and stood up. The gun stayed trained on me. The driver, a stocky woman in gray sweats, came up behind me and twisted my right arm up behind my back. I gasped in a very un-detective-like fashion and writhed to keep the pressure off my shoulder socket. It felt like my shoulder was about to pop right out of the socket.

Red Dress nodded and the brute behind me propelled me where Amanda had been taken. I glanced around quickly as we walked. I wasn't able to see much, just that we were in a warehouse of sorts, with lots of boxes stacked on metal shelves. Then I was shoved through the same door as Amanda was a moment before. She lay sprawled on the cement floor and I stumbled over her, putting my hands out to break my fall. I rolled over just as the door slammed.

I rubbed my skinned palms while I surveyed our situation. We were trapped in an empty room with stark white walls. Not a single piece of furniture, no pictures on the walls, no trash can or trash, no dust. Nothing. Except us.

Amanda stirred.

"Oh, my head," she propped herself up on one elbow and

rubbed her forehead with the other. I'd bet the combination of alcohol and chloroform was wreaking havoc on her brain. She lifted her head and saw me. She blinked and her gaze wandered around the barren room, then came back to me. "Where are we?"

I shrugged my shoulders. "Beats me."

"Did they knock you out?"

"Long enough to get me in the van. I came to during the ride, but I couldn't see anything. We're in some kind of industrial complex, that's all I could see."

She rolled over on her side and worked her way into a sitting position, leaning her back against the wall. "Well." She examined herself for a moment. "I guess I'm okay. How do we get out of here?"

"I don't know. And I'm fine, too. Thanks for asking," I said.

She glared at me. "You're the detective. Don't you know how to get us out of here? Isn't that what I hired you to do?"

"No, you hired me to find your husband, who I might add, you tried to kill. That's what got us in this mess." If looks could kill, well, you know the rest.

"I suppose you're going to add that if I wasn't drunk, we wouldn't be here." She crossed her arms defiantly.

I shook my head. "No, they were too good. They knew the layout of the country club, where the exits were, where they should be, where you would be. They had this planned very well, and they executed it well. I doubt anyone saw them take us."

"So no one knows where we are."

"Only if the FBI followed us."

Amanda sighed. "Then we're dead. You've said it yourself. This group has been successfully dodging the FBI for years." She began to tremble uncontrollably.

I sank to the floor as if I'd been punched in the stomach.

We were done for. I leaned my head back and momentarily closed my eyes. A real job sounded okay right about now, one my parents would approve of. Without warning the single over-head light winked out, plunging the room into total darkness.

"Oh, no. Reed, I don't want to die." Amanda's voice shook. "I don't want to die. I'll do anything, I'll go to jail, but I don't want to die." She began moaning softly.

I couldn't see a thing. The darkness became more sinister, enveloping us in its bleakness. I didn't know what to do. I couldn't see my hand in front of my face, so I didn't know how to even begin trying to find a way out. I heard a click and looked at the door, which swung out, away from us. A silhouette stood in the doorway, shadowed from the light behind her. She beckoned to us. I got up and helped Amanda to her feet. She was shuddering from fear, barely able to keep herself upright.

We shuffled through the door. I squinted against the sudden light. The woman in the red dress stood observing us. She aimed her gun right at my head. Behind her, the van driver, her feet spread apart in a threatening stance, had a gun trained on Amanda. And behind the driver stood two more women.

"Hold out your arms." Amanda and I did as we were told. I wasn't going to argue with a loaded gun, and Amanda didn't seem conscious of what was going on. "Cuff them." One of the women stepped forward and locked cuffs on our wrists.

"Search them." Feminine hands slid up and down our bodies, emptying our pockets of everything. My cell phone rang just as one of the women took it from my belt. She glanced at it, then hurled it forcefully into a metal trashcan. I heard the hollow rattle as it broke apart.

"Bring them over here," the woman in the red dress ordered. Her voice could've been mistaken for a man's, but the rest of her couldn't. She was tall, slender, and incredibly tan. The fash-ionable dress conformed precisely to her contours. I didn't think the Glock suited the outfit, but then, I wasn't in a position to argue. She stood aside as her companions hustled Amanda and me through a maze of stacked boxes and shelves to an open area between rows of shelves. Amanda shook so violently I could hear her teeth clanging together.

They shoved us forward unceremoniously. Two chairs waited for us.

"Sit," the woman in the red dress commanded. We sat. "Don't try anything or I'll use this." She trained the gun on me. The other women formed a half circle around us. Red Dress surveyed their handiwork, nodding with approval.

"Do something," Amanda hissed.

"Like what?" I said out of the side of my mouth.

She looked imploringly at me. I shrugged.

Red Dress barked something unintelligible at us. "No talking," she snapped. My breathing became a bit more labored. Amanda let out a squeak.

"You've really screwed things up, you know that?" Red Dress said. I wasn't sure who she was addressing, Amanda or me. "You know that?" she repeated, raising her voice. The corner of the woman's eye began twitching and her face hardened.

Amanda blanched. My mind was racing to figure a way out.

"And you should have stayed away, Mr. Ferguson," she addressed me.

"So you know my name. But who are you?" Her eyes narrowed. "You can tell me. After all, you have the gun. I'm cuffed. I'd say you have the upper hand." I was stalling for time.

"You can call me Georgia," she finally said. She focused on Amanda. "You have caused us a great deal of trouble, Mrs. Ghering. And unfortunately for you, Mr. Ferguson, she has pulled you into the situation. Regrettable, but we're going to remedy the problem now."

"But I don't understand," Amanda whimpered. "So I lied to

you. Big deal. It happens all the time. So maybe Peter wasn't as bad as I said he was. He cheated on me. Isn't that bad enough? Why should I have cared what happened to him? I paid you good money, so why should you care either?"

"We're not murderers for hire," Georgia said. I snorted at that. "No, you misunderstand our true purpose. We seek to rectify situations where justice was not done, and we're very careful to make sure that a request is worthy of our particular brand of justice."

"You're hired guns," I said derisively. "You profit from murder."

"No. The money we make supports the organization, and anything left over is donated to causes that help unfortunate women."

"Oh, right. I forgot about that. Of course it's okay, then," I said.

"You can mock me, Mr. Ferguson, but I assure you our purpose is noble. And that's why we couldn't carry out the assignment Amanda asked of us. It didn't warrant our kind of services."

"I don't get it," I said. "I thought you researched all your cases before you took something on. Why didn't you know Amanda was lying before you took her on?"

"Because I broke my own rules." A woman stepped out of the shadows behind Georgia. My jaw dropped. Amanda gulped air. And Georgia smiled knowingly.

CHAPTER TWENTY-SIX

"I broke my own rules," Maggie Delacroix repeated, coming forward. She smiled warmly at us, as if she were inviting us into her home. "It is a mistake I will not make again."

"Maggie," Amanda said breathlessly. "You said you were helping me."

"I took pity on you. A mistake I won't repeat, I assure you," Maggie said. "I believed your petty stories about Peter, how he abused you. I set the wheels in motion before I checked out what you'd said." She clasped her hands together. "As I said, it's a mistake I won't repeat."

"How can you do this?" Amanda asked. "You seem so," she searched for the word, "helpless."

"With the right resources and the determination, we can achieve anything." Maggie sounded like an ad for a Fortune 500 company. She turned to Georgia. "That was excellent work at the club. I could not have asked for a more flawless execution of a plan."

Georgia beamed. "You planned well, and your description of the club was perfect. We had no trouble at all."

"No one was the wiser," Maggie said. "Things were as usual when I left the club. No one will notice for quite some time that Amanda is gone."

I recovered from my shock. "You're the leader of the X Women?"

"Leader and founder." A hint of pride crept into her tone. "Don't be so surprised. I would not have chosen this line of work, but destiny is a funny thing."

"How can you believe what you're doing is right?"

"I am aware that many people would disagree," Maggie said. "But these women," she gestured at her minions, "were more than willing to work for the cause. And so are others. They have had tragedy in their lives. They know firsthand that our justice system is far from perfect, so they decided to make a difference."

"But why did you talk to me about your group? Weren't you afraid I would find out about your involvement?"

"I really didn't give you that much credit," she said, hurling the insult at me. "I did believe, however, that you would make good on your threat to go to the police if I didn't speak with you. I chose to try and throw you off."

"But you pointed me right to you."

"You already knew about the organization, thanks to Amanda. The matter of Derek Jones was inconsequential in the bigger scheme of our operations, which is why I chose to tell you about it."

I thought about our conversation at the club. "You felt that justice wasn't done for your daughter's friend, so you took matters into your own hands. You created the organization to have that boy killed, and you made it look like an accident. You make all your killings look like accidents. That fooled law enforcement for a long time. But are you any better than those you seek to destroy?"

"Our legal system did nothing for me. Something precious was taken away, and I wanted payment for that. An eye for an eye."

"So you set everything up to kill Derek Jones. You didn't hire anyone, did you? You used your own group." My mind was battling against pieces that didn't fit in the puzzle. "But that was only five years ago. The X Women have been around a lot longer than that. How could you have started it then?"

"The death of Derek Jones was nothing more than an execution of our services. That incident alone would never have prompted me to start the X Women. It was merely a favor for a friend."

"I don't understand," I said.

"I had something far greater taken from me. Eighteen years ago."

I thought back to our previous conversation. What had I missed? "Who was taken from you, besides Elaine Richards?"

"Her daughter," a male voice, not mine, interjected. Maggie and the other X Women whirled around. Amanda and I sat in stunned silence. A tall man walked around some boxes, edging his way to the outskirts of our little semicircle.

Maggie recovered quickly, hiding her surprise. "You are correct, Peter."

Amanda sagged in her chair, her chin resting on her chest. I stared at Peter Ghering. He stood tall, but his tense jaw and dark circles under his eyes screamed of exhaustion. He needed a shave, and his suit could've used some serious pressing, but other than that, he generally resembled the picture Amanda had shown me a week ago.

"How did you get here?" Amanda gasped.

Peter glared at Maggie. "No, let's hear what Maggie has to say. I'm as curious as you all are."

I'd been thinking about what Peter said. I turned to Maggie.

"Your daughter lives on the East Coast. She works in Washington."

"Her first daughter," Peter said. "Sally. She was kidnapped and murdered eighteen years ago. There was never a conviction."

"You had another daughter?" I stared at Maggie.

"She sure did," Peter said. "From her first marriage. Sally was eight years old, wasn't she, Maggie? Little Sally, taken from your front yard while she played."

"Did you know this?" I spat at Amanda.

She shrugged. "I think I remember some rumors about it at the club. I really didn't think it was important."

"Not important?" I nearly screeched.

"My wife pays attention to little more than the brand of vodka she's drinking," Peter said, turning to Maggie. "I, on the other hand, have golfed with Maggie's current husband. He's spoken a time or two about her first marriage, and the tragedies from it."

Maggie faced me, but her eyes focused someplace far away. "She was just a child, so innocent." Her voice cracked. "She was violated and then murdered, and her frail body thrown in the woods." She paused. "And my husband, her father, couldn't take it. He killed himself, leaving me a sizable inheritance. But my family was destroyed. Sally's murderer got away on a technicality. He roamed free while I lived in a prison. I tormented myself over what I could've done differently. And then I had a realization that I was letting her murderer kill again. My grief and anger were killing me, and it was because of Sally's murderer." She fixed her gaze on Peter again, her jaw locked determinedly. "I decided I wouldn't let that happen again. I had brains. I had money. And I wanted justice for my husband and daughter. I hired someone to take care of Sally's killer. I felt released. And I knew that others longed for justice the way I did. I am fulfilling that need."

Peter stood with his hands clenched at his sides, shaking. "You thought I deserved the same as all those others?"

"No, Peter," Maggie said. "You don't understand. Amanda talked at the club. She said you were abusive to her, that you beat her, manipulated her, controlled her. She said she feared for her life. I had little way of knowing what happened in the privacy of your home. My husband inferred that you cheated on her, that you didn't care." She shrugged. "After hearing her complaints for a while, I relented and gave her a number to call. I took pity on her, and acted before I thought about what I was doing. But when the organization realized that she was lying, we contacted the women who had taken you. I ordered them to abort the mission."

Peter's nostrils flared and his lips slid back in a snarl. He looked like a rabid wolf as he listened to Maggie. "Do you know what I've been through these last two weeks?" he yelled.

Amanda slowly raised her head, coming back to reality. "Peter, what are you doing here?" She looked completely baffled.

"What does it look like? I found the people who were trying to kill me. I didn't know what to do at first, and I didn't know who to trust. I couldn't trust you," he said to Amanda with contempt.

"But how did you know I wanted to kill you?" Amanda asked.

"It wasn't hard to figure out. I was in an airport restaurant having breakfast, and I began to feel lightheaded. I started for the bathroom and felt faint. A lady," he pointed at Georgia, "offered to help me. The next thing I know I'm blindfolded, lying on the floor of a car. I began to fight, and someone hit me over the head.

I lost consciousness again and woke up in a ditch outside of Philadelphia. After they left me for dead, I found a phone and called you. Do you remember what you said to me?" Peter turned on Amanda. "You sounded shocked and said 'You're still alive.' I knew right then you had tried to have me killed." Peter took a ragged breath. "I didn't know what to think. I didn't know who to trust, who was after me. I didn't know if I should go to the police, or if I should just show up at home." He sucked in a breath and let it out slowly. "And then I decided to come after you."

"And here you are," I murmured.

Amanda shivered.

"This is all fascinating, but we have things to attend to," Maggie interrupted.

"Don't you want to know how I ended up here?" Peter taunted her, his face an angry mask.

Maggie studied him cautiously, seeming to sense the danger in Peter's coiled fury. "Please indulge us," she said politely.

"Your organization isn't as careful as you might think. You see all these boxes," Peter pointed to the shelves around us. "They're paper boxes. Quality Paper Products. They're an office supply company. When I was in the car, before they knocked me out, I heard one of the women mention something about paper – quality paper. At first I didn't know what they meant: why would they be talking about paper? Then I realized they were talking about a business that your husband owns." He pointed to Maggie. "I've even been here myself. So I figured this company was a place to start, that it had some connection to the people who kidnapped me. I didn't know what or why, but I was going to find out. I hitchhiked all the way back, staying in cheap motels the whole time. Do you know what it feels like to bum money off of truckers and women? That's what I did. And I bought binoculars and have been down the street from here, watching this place for the past few days, so I could find out what was going on. Today I'd about given up when, to my surprise, I see a van pull into the garage with Amanda in the back seat. I had to know what was happening, so I snuck past the secretary out front. And now I know all about you and your organization." He smiled triumphantly.

"I applaud you," Maggie said. "In other circumstances we could've used your resourcefulness. As it is, we really must be moving along. I'm afraid you do know too much now. How unfortunate, when we tried to spare your life. Come, ladies. And bring our friends along. We have work to do."

Maggie turned her back on Peter, which was uncharacteristically stupid of her. Peter, functioning at a near crazed level, roared and lunged at Maggie, dragging her to the ground. The X Women around her stood frozen, shocked by Peter's actions. And then all hell broke loose.

CHAPTER TWENTY-SEVEN

Peter leaped on Maggie, cursing her as he pummeled her with his fists. The van driver and two of the women jumped into the fray, trying to pull Peter off Maggie, and at the same time avoid coming into contact with his punches. The driver's gun, body parts, and curses were flying all over the place.

Georgia seemed mesmerized by the fight. She stood unmoving, and I chose that second to hurl myself at Amanda, knocking both her and me to the ground. I felt my chair slide sideways on two legs as I tipped her chair over. It broke with a crack and we ended up in a heap of arms, legs, and chair parts. I struggled to get up, my hands still cuffed in front of me, my feet entangled in pieces of the chair and Amanda's legs. The commotion of our fall jolted Georgia out of her trance, and she stepped toward us, gun held low. Amanda crawled to her knees, yelling at me.

"You idiot," she screamed. She swung her handcuffed wrists back, clearly intent on maiming me. And Georgia stepped right into her fists, catching the backward blow in the stomach.

"Oof," Georgia groaned, buckling over. I dove at them,

laying Amanda flat on the floor, catching Georgia squarely on the knees with my shoulder. She dropped her gun and yelled in pain as her legs bowed back in an unnatural way. I finished the tackle, sending her into a fall. Her head slammed on the hard cement floor with a sickening thud.

"Get off me!" I heard Amanda shouting from under me. I scrambled to retrieve Georgia's gun, clutching at it as I scooted across the floor. I grabbed the gun with both hands, rolled over into a sitting position, and pointed the gun toward the general melee before me. I saw two of the X Women piled on the floor, bucking to and fro, Peter's feet and arms protruding from under the heap. Maggie stood a few feet away, her dress torn at one shoulder, her lip bleeding and one eye swelling up, her usually perfect hair flying in any number of directions. Another X Woman used one hand to pull Maggie farther back from the pile. The X Woman waved the other hand around, her gun pointing randomly at the pile, at Amanda, and at me.

I pointed my gun at her. "Stop!" I yelled.

What happened next seemed like a movie playing frame by frame. The van driver turned her head and looked at me, surprise crossing her face when she saw my gun aimed at her. Maggie's mouth opened slowly and she yelled "noooo...". The other woman raised her gun, her arm wavering slowly. Then I was looking into that gaping black hole from where a bullet would emerge and kill me. I gritted my teeth and pulled the trigger of my gun, my eyes closing involuntarily. I heard an explosion, and at the same time I lurched to my right. As I tumbled, I heard another explosion, and a stinging sensation on my backside. I ended up on my elbows and knees, dropping the gun. It skittered a few feet away. I heard a third explosion, and screams. I ducked my head, aware that my elbows and knees hurt. Then the movie slipped into fast forward.

I opened my eyes and saw the woman sagging onto the

floor. Her gun slipped from her hand and she clutched at her left shoulder, where a red spot grew out of her white shirt. Maggie bent over her, trying to see where the bullet had gone. Amanda whimpered as she cowered behind the chair that hadn't broken. I scrambled over and retrieved the gun, giving Georgia a wide berth. I didn't need to; she lay unmoving where she'd fallen and struck her head. As I stood up, my rear hurt, even though I'd fallen on my face. I began to tremble as I leveled the gun with my cuffed hands at the X Women.

"Freeze!" I shouted, hoping my command would be more effective this time.

To my surprise, the movie paused. Everyone stopped and stared at me. The pile of X Women and Peter quit bucking, and even Amanda grew quiet. The gun wavered in my hands. Sweat trickled into my eyes and I heaved for breath. I wasn't sure what to do next.

"Everybody freeze!" Everyone looked around in confusion. I hadn't said a word. Then who...?

Agents Forbes and White came running around the corner, guns held high. A small army of agents followed them, spreading out among us. Some descended on the X Women, yanking the two off of Peter, while others subdued Maggie and the wounded X Woman, both of whom put up little protest.

"Are you all right?" Forbes asked me. I stared at him. "Reed, are you okay?" he asked again. He eased my gun down and grasped me by the shoulders, studying me cautiously.

I took a second to realize who was talking to me. "Yeah. I'm okay."

"Good," Forbes said, letting me go. "We thought we were too late." He turned to the action going on behind his back.

"Hey. Where the hell were you five minutes ago?" I barked at him. "Do you always wait until the work is done to show up?"

He turned around and gave me a stern look, but his eyes

sparkled. "We got here as soon as we could. If you hadn't been so intent on losing us, it would've been sooner. As it was, we had to do some quick work. We thought you all were taken to Maggie's house, but when we didn't find anyone there, we came right here. We were talking with the front desk lady when we heard the shots and came running."

Amanda peeked from around the chair. "It's about time someone came to my rescue." She stood up unsteadily.

"You might not think that after we book you," Forbes said.

"What?" The innocent look on her face didn't fool anyone.

"At least you're alive," Agent White said. "Isn't that what you wanted? You'll face the music now." Amanda grimaced, but she couldn't argue with her own words.

My body was screaming at me, sore in too many places to count. "I feel lightheaded." I blinked hard at Forbes.

"Hey, buddy, you're bleeding." White, who had been helping with the other X Women, pointed at me.

I began examining myself, but didn't see anything.

"No, back there."

I craned my neck around, exploring my backside with my hands. "Oh, man! She shot me in the butt?" I couldn't believe it, but it was true. My rear end suddenly hurt like nobody's business.

Agent Forbes tried to hide a smile. And then I fainted.

CHAPTER TWENTY-EIGHT

Everything was white. Puffy white clouds surrounded me. I had wings. And a harp. What? Was this what it was like when you died? But I'd only been shot in the rear. That wasn't life-threatening, was it? I saw a tunnel and white light coming at me. I opened my eyes.

Agent White had his prodigious face inches from me. "So, you're awake." He leaned down at me, and I smelled his onion breath.

I was lying on my side, facing away from the door. My whole body ached, but especially a certain area underneath bandages and tape that I couldn't see. I swallowed and my throat felt like sandpaper. I glanced around. Everything was white. White light shining through white curtains, white sheets on the bed. And Agent White sitting there. How appropriate.

"Yeah," I croaked at White. I was definitely awake.

"Good. Maybe you can tell us why you ignored a specific order to stay away from Amanda Ghering." He took a seat on a wooden chair with a plastic seat cushion. The chair squeaked under his bulk, the cushion hissing loudly.

I left his question unanswered, more concerned about my well-being. I felt like crap, and I wasn't sure how I got here, wherever here was. I knew who I was, who the President was, and I thought I knew what day it was. Did they ask anything else when they wanted to find out if you were oriented? I began to check out my injuries. An IV-tube ran from my left arm to a bag of clear liquid hanging from a metal pole. I reached over with my other arm to a rolling table for a water pitcher the color of puke. I managed to pour myself a glass, groaning from the exertion. Agent White crossed his arms over his massive chest, apparently too disgusted with me to lend a helping hand. My elbows were scraped and bruised, and as I moved my legs, I knew that my knees must be in the same condition. I took a long gulp of tepid water, the sandy feeling in my throat subsiding.

"So?"

"What time is it?"

He didn't bother looking at his watch. "After five. Why did you keep working on the case?"

I lay back on my side, with a pile of white pillows propped under my right shoulder and head. "I wanted to finish it," I said.

I heard the door open and shut, and Special Agent Forbes came around the bed and into my line of sight. "You've had quite a day," he said. It didn't sound friendly, but then it didn't sound unfriendly either. He leaned against the window ledge, put his hands in his pockets and examined me. "How do you feel?"

I squinted at him. "Like I got rear-ended by a truck," I said. "Muscles I didn't even know I had are sore."

"You're lucky that bullet didn't hit somewhere else, or you might be in more trouble. As it is, you should be grateful you have as much muscle there as you do."

"Don't hold back," I grimaced. "You can tell me I have a fat butt."

Forbes actually smiled at that. "You're going to be just fine. They removed the bullet and patched you up, and that muscle will be sore for a while. You lost some blood, too, but you'll be back on your feet in no time." I stayed silent, waiting for the punchline. "The doctors want to keep you overnight for observation. They're going to release you in the morning."

He stopped talking. I waited a moment, then said, "What?"

"I need you to come down to our offices, so we can wrap things up." He pulled out his wallet and extracted a business card, handing it to me.

I reached out a hand and took it. I read the address on it and set it on the table. I sucked in a breath and held it for a second. I looked at White, who frowned at me, then at Forbes, who waited for me to speak. "The suspense is killing me. Why don't you tell me now what kind of trouble I'm in?"

"Okay," Forbes agreed. "You realize you interfered with a federal investigation." It seemed a rhetorical question, so I remained silent. "You could've ruined a lot of work for a lot of people."

"That's right," White began. Forbes held up a hand and White clamped his jaw shut.

"I'm sure we don't need to discuss the details of your mistakes," Forbes said, "or how dangerous it was to continue. I think you're sufficiently paying for that now." He distinctly did not look at my wound. "And you did in fact help bring down the leader of the X Women. That warrants special consideration."

"Thank you very much," I said, maybe with a bit too much sarcasm.

"Hey, we saved your butt," White leaned closer to me, his index finger jabbing at me.

"Excuse me, but if you saved my butt, I wouldn't be here," I shot back at him.

"Gentlemen," Forbes interrupted. "Wayne," he said to White. "Maybe you should get yourself a cup of coffee." White composed himself, gave me a last severe glare, stood up, and left the room.

"I'd say he's more upset with your actions than I am." Forbes came over by the bed. "Listen, Reed. You're in trouble here." I started to protest, but he continued. "Look, I'm not happy that you got in the way, but in the end you did help. If you cooperate with us, tell us what you know, testify against these women if need be, maybe I can make sure that nothing happens to you."

"What happened to the woman I shot?"

"She's being treated, but she'll be okay. You managed to take her out of action, but leave her alive. We couldn't have trained someone better. Lucky shot?" he asked with amusement.

"Something like that." I looked down and breathed with relief. I didn't want to have to live with killing someone.

"Having everyone alive makes things a lot less complicated. My offer stands."

"I walk away, no charges against me?" I asked.

He nodded. "I'll see what I can do. Come down to my office tomorrow, and we'll get a statement from you, and have you fill out some paperwork. There's always paperwork." He sighed.

"I'll be there," I said. "By the way, what happened after I fainted?"

"I never saw anybody hit the ground so fast." He grinned. "We arrested all the women, and we've tracked down the fake FBI agents and arrested them as well. Maggie, now there's a woman of vengeance. She's not telling us a thing. She's asked for a lawyer and is already preparing her defense." His eyes narrowed in anger. "We're trying to get the others to talk, to turn on each other. We've gotten a few leads from the warehouse, but it'll take some time to track all the women down. I'm sure a lot of them are already on the run."

"And Peter?"

"Peter was treated for some bumps and bruises, and released. We questioned him for quite a while, and that's only the start." Forbes shook his head. "He's had one helluva week, scrounging around, hiding like a criminal himself. If he would've called the police, or us, he could've avoided a lot."

"He didn't trust the police, or anyone else."

Forbes shrugged. "We're not all bad." He paused. "Peter will be okay. He'll have a great story to tell his grandkids."

I snorted. "Yeah, how his ex-wife tried to have him killed. I'm sure that'll replace Dr. Seuss."

"Okay, he can tell it at the club."

"And Amanda?"

"She is alive and well, and in custody. She'll face charges for conspiring to kill her husband, and any other charge we can come up with. You got what you wanted on that one."

"Excuse me?"

"You didn't let her die, but she'll spend a good long time behind bars."

"Oh," I said. He seemed to have all my bugged conversations memorized.

Forbes stuck out his hand. "You did well, my friend. If I can return the favor..."

I awkwardly shook his hand, totally surprised. "I figured you'd want to throw the book at me, since I interfered with your investigation."

Forbes cocked his head. "I'll get over it." He winked at me and left the room.

I rolled back until my rear hit the pillows behind me and the pain stopped me. It wasn't that bad, really. A pain in the rear, I thought wryly.

I chuckled to myself, closed my eyes, and drifted into a calm sleep.

CHAPTER TWENTY-NINE

Monday morning came with a chill in the air, but bright sunshine. After a day and a half in the hospital, I was ready to leave. At nine, Ace and Bob showed up. I had arranged the night before for Ace to pick me up because he had the day off, but I was surprised to see Bob tagging along.

"Hey, dude," Ace said as he followed Bob into the room. Okay, so Ace was tagging along. He nervously played with the corner of his coat, his eyes darting around the room. "Are you going to be okay?"

I had gotten up when the nurse brought in my breakfast tray. After picking at some runny eggs and dry toast, I had showered carefully, taking extra caution with the scrapes on my elbows, knees, hands, and especially my bandaged rear end. I dressed in a pair of sweats and a sweater that Deuce brought over the previous evening, and combed my wet hair into some semblance of order.

The doctor told me that with the exception of a scar in a place where few people would see it, I would recover just fine.

My release papers had been signed and I was sitting gingerly on the edge of the bed when Bob and Ace came for me.

"You don't look too bad," Bob said. "Are you ready?"

I glanced at Ace, who was doing everything he could to pretend like he wasn't in a hospital room, running a hand through his ponytail. "Yeah, let's go before your brother dies of fright."

Bob smiled. "He'll be okay. Ace, grab his bag." Ace picked up the brown paper bag that contained the clothes I'd worn when I was admitted. The nurse had brought it to me this morning. The crumpled pair of jeans was now suitable for the trash; the seat of the pants had a dark reddish brown stain on it, and a hole that I could put my thumb through.

A nurse entered the room, pushing a wheelchair. "Your ride is here, Mr. Ferguson," she greeted us cheerfully.

"Is that necessary?" I asked. I was wounded, not crippled.

"Hospital rules." The smile on her face didn't budge.

I shrugged and limped over to the wheelchair and sat down, putting all my weight on my right side. She wheeled me out of the room to the elevator, and in five minutes, she deposited me on the passenger seat of Bob's car. Ace, decidedly calmer now that we were outside of the hospital, chattered the whole ride over to the Colorado Bureau of Investigations, where Agent Forbes had a temporary office. Ace mostly wanted to know if the fight I was in was anything like the one at the end of *The Big Sleep*. He seemed disappointed when I said it wasn't.

I arranged to call Bob on his cell phone when I finished, and I walked as normally as I could manage into the building. After two hours of being interviewed by Agent Forbes and his team, I was exhausted, but pleased that Forbes had kept his word. I cooperated, and the FBI didn't press charges against me. Agent Forbes wanted another meeting, so we scheduled that, and then I called Bob.

When we arrived back at the condo, Bob and Ace were kind enough to help me upstairs and into my place. They rearranged the furniture in the living room so that I could lie on my belly on the couch and see the television without craning my neck. It wasn't the most comfortable position, but it protected my sensitive derrière. Ace fixed me a sandwich and a glass of Coke, completed with a straw for easy drinking.

"You need anything else?" Bob asked.

"A couple of aspirin." My rear hurt.

Ace scooted into the kitchen and returned with a bottle. I took two greedily.

"Anything else?" Bob asked again.

"No, I'm fine now. Thanks for everything."

"Here's the phone," Ace said, putting the cordless down on the coffee table. "You call if you need anything. We're right downstairs, so it's easy to get here."

Bob and I exchanged an amused look. "Thanks, Ace. That's good to know."

"We'll check on you later," Bob said. "Don't worry about anything."

"I won't."

They left and I soon drifted off while the television played Ace's favorite movie, *The Terminator*. The phone rang, waking me. "Hello," I mumbled into the phone. On the television screen, Arnold was doing some nasty surgery on his electronic eye. Cool scene.

"Where have you been?" Cal asked, more than a little concern in his voice. "I've been calling you since yesterday morning. You're not going to believe what I found out."

"It's been a helluva day or two," I said. "You won't believe what I've been through."

"Yeah? Well, remember that list I gave you, with the accidental deaths?" He didn't wait for a response, but barreled on ahead. "One of them related to a little girl named Sally Hanson. Guess who that is?"

"The daughter of Maggie Delacroix," I said. I heard complete silence on the other end of the phone.

"How did you know that?" Cal demanded finally.

"Have I got a story for you," I said, and proceeded to relate the events of the last twenty-four hours, complete with my theory of the setup, and its relation to *The Big Sleep*, and my not-so-detective-like wound in the butt. Cal roared with laughter after I assured him that the wound was far from deadly, or even serious.

"I'm impressed, Reed. You actually managed to solve your first case. Successfully, I might add. You put the pieces together just like Bogie. Life imitating art."

"Or something like that. Now maybe I can convince my dad that I have a real job."

"I doubt that," Cal said. "But you have my vote."

"I couldn't have done it without you."

"Hey, I didn't do very much. I'll help anytime you want, as long as I can stay in my own home."

"Always," I laughed as I hung up. What would I do without Cal? I turned my attention back to the movie, but quickly drifted off again. I was dreaming of Arnold and Bogie when the doorbell rang. The television illuminated the room in pastel blue. I'd been asleep for a while this time.

"Door's open," I hollered, wondering why Ace didn't let himself in.

"How are you feeling?" Willie's soft voice drifted through the dimness.

"Hey," I said, trying to sit up.

"No, stay there." Willie came into the room and sat on the edge of the coffee table. "You doing okay?"

Much better since you're here, I thought. "Where's your boyfriend?"

"I'm not sure. I think he and I are finished. But it's okay." She smiled at me. "Do you need anything?"

"No," I said. "But the company's nice."

"Are you okay? I mean, with the boyfriend thing?"

"Uh huh." She smiled again. "Really, I am."

"Okay." She did seem fine, so I let it go.

Willie picked up *The Big Sleep* DVD. "This one looks interesting. Want to watch it?"

"Sure." I was just glad she wanted to stay. And I was impressed that she wanted to watch an old detective story. Maybe this recuperation wouldn't be as bad as I had thought.

She slid off the coffee table and inserted the DVD into the player. Right then the phone rang.

"You want me to leave?" Willie asked.

I shook my head. Willie watched the movie as I picked up the phone.

"Hello, dear. It's Mother."

"Hi, Mom." I yawned. "How are you?"

"I'm fine, dear. I just wanted to remind you about our flight. I don't want you to forget. Are you okay? It sounds like you were asleep. Were you taking a nap? And in the middle of the day. I thought you were working. You know your father didn't think you could make a go of this detective thing."

"I'm still working, Mom. I'm still a detective." I felt groggy. I turned gingerly on my side, careful of my wounded butt. I rolled my eyes at Willie, wishing I could hang up on my mother.

My mother harrumphed at me. "That's nice, dear. I just want you to be happy. I only wish you would pick something a little less dangerous. Goodness, what if someone tries to shoot you? I don't know what I would do then. You know that the shows, like that *Murder, She Wrote,* aren't at all realistic. That Angela Lansbury always comes out smelling like a rose. Really."

I made a quick decision: now was definitely *not* the time to tell her about getting shot in the ass. I could tell her about finishing my first case, and my not-so-near brush with death, when they visited for the holidays. When she could see for herself that I was perfectly fine.

"You really sound terrible, dear," she continued, barely taking a breath. "Are you sure you're okay? You sound funny, like you did the other day. You're not doing drugs, are you?"

I chuckled. "No, Mother."

———

**Turn the page for an excerpt from *Reel Estate Rip-Off,*
Reed Ferguson mystery book 2!**

SNEAK PEEK

Reel Estate Rip-Off, Reed Ferguson Mysteries, book 2

"Arnold Schwarzenegger is the greatest actor ever!"

Ace Smith stood just inside the doorway of my office, glaring at his brother, Deuce. The opening shot of a long-standing argument between the Goofball Brothers had been delivered.

"Dude, Sly is way better." Deuce's lips curled in a half-grin at his older brother. Then Deuce gestured for me to hurry up.

"Bruce Willis is better than Sly." Ace grabbed a pen from my desk and began waving it like a sword. He had a triumphant look on his baby face.

"He doesn't even do action movies," Deuce said, rolling his eyes.

"Hello! Can you say *Die Hard?* One of the best pictures ever," Ace said.

"Better than *The Terminator?* No way!" Deuce advanced into the room, snatched a pencil off the desk, and held it up.

"Hold on." Ace spread his arms like a referee keeping two boxers, or in this case, jousters, apart. "Let's ask Reed. He's knows movies. And he's a detective."

I turned my head in surprise. It was true. I was a movie buff. And a detective. But I had been sitting at my desk, trying to ignore the interchange while listening to a voice mail message. I didn't want to get involved.

"Yeah, Reed. What do you think?" Deuce asked.

No one ever won this argument, which was why it still continued. I hung up the phone, and shrugged my shoulders to indicate my indifference. I didn't care. "You know what my vote is."

"Oh yeah. Henry Bogart," Ace said, pointing the pen at me. "All that *film now* stuff. That Bogart guy is dead, you know, so that doesn't count."

"It's *Humphrey* Bogart and *film noir*," I corrected him with a laugh, pointing at a framed Bogart movie poster of *The Big Sleep* on the wall. "And Bogie can act circles around any of your guys." I pocketed my keys and led them out to the small waiting room.

"Talking golf again," Deuce joked. They both laughed. It was a hot, dry Friday afternoon in August. The temperature in downtown Denver was hovering in the mid-90's, perfect conditions for a few cold ones during happy hour. I had decided to call it a day early and had phoned the brothers, who were available at that time of day because they were ending a week of vacation. Now we were heading over to B 52's, a local pool hall, and I was heading into the weekend. No work until Monday. Actually, I'd wrapped up a case a week ago, and hadn't done much since. Famous last words.

I shooed the brothers out the door and was locking it behind me when I heard another voice, distinctly un-Goofball-like.

"Reed Ferguson?" Each word was enunciated carefully, a clipped tone.

I turned. The ghost of Burt Lancaster gazed back at me. "Swede?"

"Excuse me?" A confused expression spread across the man's face. Okay, not slick on my part, but he was the spitting image of Lancaster in his film debut as Swede Andersen in *The Killers*, a classic noir film. Same face, same perfectly coiffed dark hair with the wavy curls, same dark, chilling eyes. Except that Swede Andersen wouldn't be wearing a three-piece suit and Gucci loafers. And right now the eyes were dimmed by a look of sadness.

"Has anyone ever told you you look like Burt Lancaster?"

The confused look on his face vanished, replaced by annoyance. "A time or two," he said, his jaw tightening.

"Never mind," I said. Behind him, the Goofball Brothers stared at me impatiently, shifting around like two little boys who needed to pee really badly. "I'm Reed."

He shook my hand firmly, all business. "Jack Healy. I've caught you at a bad time," he said by way of an apology, though I detected no hint of sorrow in his voice.

I gestured toward the guys. "We were heading out, but I can spare you a few minutes." Behind Jack Healy, Ace started waving his hands in a "no way" gesture, while Deuce looked crestfallen. They had already been antsy to leave. Was I going to have the nerve to ask them to wait longer?

"Why don't you guys go on, and I'll catch up with you later." I may be crazy, but I wasn't stupid. If I had the brothers wait in my office, within two minutes they'd be arguing and fighting like ten-year-olds. *That* would make a good impression on a prospective client.

They both relaxed visibly, goofy smiles on their goofy faces. "We'll see you there," Ace called as they hurried off down the hall.

"Thank you," Jack said, throwing a hesitant look at the retreating brothers.

I opened the door and escorted Jack into the inner office.

He took a seat across from my desk and waited until I had settled into a chair, my elbows leaning on the desk, giving him the best attention I could muster for a Friday afternoon right before happy hour.

"I'm sorry to bother you right before the weekend," he began. And again, I didn't think he sounded sorry at all. He looked more irritated, like he thought I shouldn't be leaving my office before five o'clock. If he only knew the erratic hours I kept. Ah, the life of a detective. "I took off work early to swing by your office, so I really wanted to be sure I saw you today," Jack continued. "I can't afford to take the time at all, but it seems necessary." He hesitated, glanced at his watch, then back at me. "I want to hire you."

Obviously, considering he was here, I chose to think.

Jack paused to gather his thoughts. Then he leaned forward in the chair. "I want to hire you to find my brother's killer. Or killers."

I stared back at him. "You've got my attention."

His gaze seemed to say, "About time." "I suppose I should start at the beginning," was what he did say.

"That would be good."

And so he did, loosening his tie as he talked. "My brother Ned was killed a month ago. He fell while cycling in the mountains. We think he lost control of his bike and ended up over the side of a cliff." I vaguely remembered seeing something about that on the news, but kept silent. Jack sighed. "He broke his neck in the fall and was killed instantly." A pained look crossed his face, and he stopped.

I waited a beat before saying, "I don't understand. How could there be a killer or killers if your brother fell? It sounds more like a terrible accident."

"I don't believe it happened that way." Jack glared at me with grim determination. "The police ruled it an accident. The autopsy indicated that Ned was drunk and on barbiturates and didn't know what he was doing, but I know better."

"How?"

"First of all, Ned didn't drink much, and he didn't do drugs. And he never went cycling. He hated being in the mountains, hated driving on the winding roads. He wouldn't have gone up there, and certainly not when he was drunk."

"Where did this happen?"

"Outside of Buena Vista. There's a trail that runs near Mount Princeton. They found his car parked at a trail head. He died on a Saturday but his body wasn't found for three days. There's no way anyone will convince me that he went there alone, or willingly. Not Ned."

I contemplated Jack's straightforward gaze. He seemed sure about what he was saying. "How can you be so certain that your brother wouldn't go cycling, or that he could fall while doing it? That could happen to any of us."

"Ned was afraid of heights. Pathologically afraid. He never went cycling, hiking, climbing, or anything like that in the mountains. He wouldn't even sit by a window in a high-rise building."

This piqued my interest. "The police checked into this, right?"

He nodded, chewing at his lower lip. "Sure. But everything pointed to it being ruled exactly like they said. There wasn't a shred of evidence to make them think differently."

"Did you tell them your suspicions?"

"Yes. But with the evidence they had, they said they concluded that accidents happen." He picked at the perfect crease in his trousers as he talked. "They dropped it. But I know it couldn't have happened that way. If I have to pay someone myself to find out the truth, I'll do it." He stopped with the pant leg and looked up at me. "Are you willing to find out what happened to my brother?"

I did a quick mental inventory of my schedule in my head. Nothing coming up. Last case finished a week ago. I'd spent more time playing pool in the last seven days than I had in months, and my game still wasn't very good. I'd never solve the Best Actor argument with the Goofball Brothers. "I'll take it," I said.

"Sounds good." Sounding just like Burt Lancaster.

———

Continue reading
Reel Estate Rip-Off: **reneepawlish.com/REwb**

OR

Sign up for my newsletter, and receive book 2 in the Reed Ferguson mystery series, *Reel Estate Rip-Off* as a welcome gift!

Click here to get started:
reneepawlish.com/R2D1

FREE BOOK

Sign up for my newsletter, and receive book 2 in the Reed Ferguson mystery series, *Reel Estate Rip-Off* as a welcome gift! You'll also receive another bonus!

Click here to get started:
reneepawlish.com/R2D1

RENÉE'S BOOKSHELF

Reed Ferguson Mysteries:
This Doesn't Happen In The Movies
Reel Estate Rip-Off
The Maltese Felon
Farewell, My Deuce
Out Of The Past
Torch Scene
The Lady Who Sang High
Sweet Smell Of Sucrets
The Third Fan
Back Story
Night of the Hunted
The Postman Always Brings Dice
Road Blocked
Small Town Focus
Nightmare Sally
The Damned Don't Die
Double Iniquity
The Lady Rambles

A Killing

Reed Ferguson Novellas:
Ace in the Hole
Walk Softly, Danger

Reed Ferguson Short Stories:
Elvis And The Sports Card Cheat
A Gun For Hire
Cool Alibi
The Big Steal
The Wrong Woman

Dewey Webb Historical Mystery Series:
Web of Deceit
Murder In Fashion
Secrets and Lies
Honor Among Thieves
Trouble Finds Her
Mob Rule
Murder At Eight

Dewey Webb Short Stories:
Second Chance
Double Cross

Standalone Psychological Suspense:
What's Yours Is Mine
The Girl in the Window

The Sarah Spillman Mysteries:
Deadly Connections
Deadly Invasion

Deadly Guild
Coming Early 2021

The Sarah Spillman Mystery Short Stories:
Seven for Suicide
Saturday Night Special
Dance of the Macabre

Supernatural Mystery:
Nephilim Genesis of Evil

Short Stories:
Take Five Collection
Codename Richard: A Ghost Story
The Taste of Blood: A Vampire Story

Nonfiction:
The Sallie House: Exposing the Beast Within

CHILDREN'S BOOKS
Middle-grade Historical Fiction:
This War We're In

The Noah Winter Adventure Series:
The Emerald Quest
Dive into Danger
Terror On Lake Huron

ABOUT THE AUTHOR

Renée Pawlish is the author of The Reed Ferguson mystery series, *Nephilim Genesis of Evil*, The Noah Winter adventure series for young adults, *Take Five*, a short story collection that includes a Reed Ferguson mystery, and The *Sallie House: Exposing the Beast Within*, about a haunted house investigation in Kansas.

Renée loves to travel and has visited numerous countries around the world. She has also spent many summer days at her parents' cabin in the hills outside of Boulder, Colorado, which was the inspiration for the setting of Taylor Crossing in her novel *Nephilim*.

Visit Renée at www.reneepawlish.com.

 facebook.com/reneepawlish.author

 twitter.com/ReneePawlish

 instagram.com/reneepawlish_author

Made in United States
Orlando, FL
29 August 2022